PERSIAN
BRIDES

PERSIAN BRIDES

a novel by
Dorit Rabinyan

Translated from the Hebrew by Yael Lotan

GEORGE BRAZILLER PUBLISHER
NEW YORK

First published in the United States in 1998 by George Braziller, Inc.

Originally published in Hebrew in 1995 by Am Oved Publishing House

© 1995 by Dorit Rabinyan and Am Oved Publishing House

English translation © 1998 by the Institute for the Translation of Hebrew Literature

For information, please address the publisher:

George Braziller, Inc.
171 Madison Avenue
New York, NY 10016

Library of Congress Cataloging-in-Publication Data:

Rabinyan, Dorit
    [Simtat ha-shekediyot be-Omerig'an. English]
    Persian brides / Dorit Rabinyan ; translated by Yael Lotan.
        p.   cm.
    ISBN 0-8076-1430-0 (hardcover)
    I. Lotan, Yael, 1935–   . II. Title.
    PJ5054.R257S5613 1998
    892.4'36—dc21   97-45493
                                    CIP

Designed by Rita Lascaro
Printed and bound in the United States
First edition

CONTENTS

Part One

THE NIGHT
OF THE
WATERMELON

CHAPTER ONE

That night Flora wanted to eat watermelon. She had started to cry earlier in the evening, when she sat with Nazie in the kitchen, fatter than she had ever been, her tears, too, fatter than ever. But then she cried not for a watermelon but for her husband. Nazie could no longer bear to see Flora crying so hard and fetched her the big cushion embroidered with white swans from the parlor. Flora took a deep breath before resting her palms on the floor and, raising her big bottom in the air, signaled with her eyes to Nazie to hurry and shove the cushion under it. The pair of white swans vanished under her heavy body, and her dress spread over them. She rested her back against the scarred kitchen wall, clutched once more her swelling belly between her hands, and wept fat tears. Nazie, too, slid down from the worn cane stool and sat on the cold stone floor, her little legs somewhat splayed, her anklebones as angular as little elbows.

Into the cloth bowl formed by the wide skirt between her legs, Nazie poured all at once hundreds of bitter white rice grains. Her eyes narrowed at the sight of the green mildew that had spread through them because of the dampness in the bean shed. She lowered her head, letting her plaits fall between her thighs, the better to see the damaged and infected grains, and the tiny stones and winged insects that had sneaked into the rice bag pretending to be innocent grains. With supple and skillful fingers, the fingers of an eleven-year-old who bit her nails to the rosy quick, Nazie picked out the good rustling grains and put them in the cooking pot. The bad, squeaky grains she gathered in her sweaty fist and tossed them every now and then into the mouth of the oven, where they danced and crackled on the ever-glowing embers until they fell silent.

Flora was fifteen years old, four years older than Nazie, and this was her first pregnancy. All the village women who emerged, veiled and pinned, from their sooty kitchens nodded their chins in agreement, closed their black eyes firmly, and compressed their lips. They all admitted that they had not seen such a difficult pregnancy as Flora Ratoryan's for a long time, unless you count Mamou the whore's impregnation by the king of the village demons, whose sprouting seed was sharpening her belly into a hump, and who knows what will come out of it before long, they sighed, and God preserve us from any more of these *kuchik madar*, little mother, pregnancies. Nazie had also heard that all these troubles had fallen upon the village because the night that Flora became pregnant was a cursed night of a lunar eclipse, when even hens lay rotten blood-red eggs. The strict ban on impregnating virgin brides, let alone very young ones, on such a malevolent night, when souls tremble in dread and babies shriek in their sleep, was known to all men, except to Shahin Bozidozi, the short, thin-haired cloth merchant who married Flora.

10

Six months had passed, starting in the spring and ending in the early winter, since the day Shahin entered Omerijan through the itinerants' gate, his arm broken, his garments shredded by wanderings, stinking of long-fermented donkey's piss. He had started out from his native town Babol, on the shore of the Caspian Sea, a town whose men are crooks and whose women are flighty, heading for the petroleum harbor of the southern city Abadan. As poor and dishonest as when he had left, he returned on his long-eared ass to the northern villages, where, according to his father, lived the simplest and most honest Jews of the country. On his way north he stopped in Tehran, where he encountered a splendid ambassadorial procession held in honor of the king, Reza Shah Pahlavi. Thousands of soldiers in glittering uniforms lined the main street leading from Medan a-Safa to the Gulistan Palace, the site of the "golden throne," the royal seat that the king had brought from his journeys in India. Behind the rows of soldiers thronged the subjects of the king, among them Jews, Armenians, and fire-worshipping Zoroastrians, led by their communal leaders holding burning candles and joining the crowds in songs of praise for the king and his ministers. Shahin recognized the opportunity, veiled his squinting eye, and seduced a girl apprentice from the royal tailor's workshop in the Shamsol Amera Palace in the city square. The girl, who had gaps in her teeth and pins stuck in her garments, led him through the maze of sewing workrooms, and when she was caught, she was led out to be hanged.

In his flight from the palace cellars Shahin removed from the shoulders of a headless dummy a handsome velvet cloak that the royal tailor and his assistants had been sewing for the king's son. It was made up of three layers of scarlet cloth, with the royal lion, holding a brace of swords in its mouth while the sun rose behind its back, embroidered in gold on its collar and cuffs. Shahin used his merchant's scissors to mutilate the cape, and the cloth he sold sufficed for holiday gowns for four far-from-thin women and one girl-child of good family. But the golden swords that had been crossed by an artist and placed in the lion's maw betrayed the theft from the palace, and the five vain females were eventually hanged along with the little seamstress, still wearing their scarlet gowns.

While they were being led to the gallows, the scarlet trains trailing on their heels, Shahin reached Omerijan where, washed and shaved and smelling of kerosene, he married Flora Ratoryan the poulterer's daughter, impregnated her, and disappeared without a backward glance. He left her a baby in her belly and lice in her hair. He journeyed as far as the villages around the city of Isfahan, whose red-cheeked apples have a sweet intoxicating aroma, and assured the notoriously foolish villagers that the cheap Persian silk in his bags had been smuggled in slave ships from India, and to prove it, he would leap from side to side, chanting songs in Hindi, his walleye rolling this way and that. Clenching his teeth, he had promised that at the end of two round spring months he would return with a good income to his giggling new wife, who smelled of honey like her beekeeper grandparents, and who had a mole in the hollow of her throat like a drop of chocolate that had fallen there from her greedy mouth. Two months, he said, or at the most three, and he thrust out his square jaw, promising to bring her rosy Isfahan apples. But since then a savagely hot summer had passed, sprawled like a black veil over the village, and still Shahin did not return to the village whose houses stood close together, like the stalled carriages of an engineless train.

Down from the villages of the Alborz range to the northern coastal plain marched golden and orange camels, carrying on their backs merchants and itinerant peddlers whose minds had become addled, their turbans as ragged as their shoes, and in their mouths rumors as hollow as their teeth. Speaking in an ancient Persian dialect originating in sun-and-citrus-rich Shiraz, they told of a deceitful young cloth merchant from Babol, whose return was awaited by three young brides and one widow, all of them pregnant. They told also of a Bokharan girl he had left intact, who in her despair drowned herself in a bog, whispering the meaning of his name in her mother tongue. But since they could not agree if it was his right or his left eye that squinted, Flora preferred to believe that it was not her husband they were talking about. Seeing that she doubted their stories, they lavished praise on his charms and his high shoulders and fell into the trap they had dug with their tongues. Flora's mother chased them from her house, cursing the wicked rumormongers who crushed hearts like eggshells. But like the dead Bokharan girl, whose hair floated on the black muck, Flora was unable to chase their words from her hungry heart.

* * *

"Why isn't my husband coming, Nazie? Why? Why?...," Flora mumbled on the kitchen floor, swaying from side to side, her bottom revealing alternately the snowy neck of one swan and the tail of the other. She lifted the wide hem of her dress to wipe her tears and to fan herself between the thighs. She blew her congested nose on the corner of the chador, the great half-moon cloth shawl that she wrapped around the shoulders, forehead, and chin, exposing only her lovely eyes, nose, and lips, whose curves, the villagers said, invited kisses. When she cried, her teeth also showed, not standing in two orderly rows but climbing over each other in a heap, as if they, too, wanted to burst from her mouth with the moaned words, which they graced with the ivory gleam of her laughter and smiles. She slapped her great golden-brown thighs with the outspread palm of her hand, leaving red stamps on the skin of her crossed legs, drawing the pain from her heart.

Nazie saw Flora sunk in grief, and her heart went out to her cousin. For a moment she considered telling Flora what she had heard in the bathhouse regarding the lunar eclipse, to console her by blaming the heavenly bodies, but she desisted before opening her mouth. Her orphan existence had taught her that no excuses, not even involving all the stars that twinkled over the roof, could dispel the pain of loneliness. Holding the slipping ends of the chador to her hidden chin with one hand, Nazie rubbed the rice grains with the knuckles of the other. She liked the cool feel of the grains. Dry and free of mildew and insects, their rustling was sharp and clear and overcame Flora's wails. But when they swelled in the boiling water on the range, and doubled their bulk and grew sweet and white, then they were as quiet as Flora was in sleep.

Nazie could have sworn by her dead mother and father that even in the month of Nisan the previous year, when Flora's older brother Moussa locked her in the house because she kept laughing and eating and forbade her to go out and meet people from the eve of Passover to the feast of Shavuot, and Flora became as thin and yellow as a stalk of wheat, she had not looked as wretched as she did now. In her longings Flora scarified the flesh of her cheeks with her fingernails, and the scratches that ran from her temples to her chin, having healed blue and purple, opened anew and reddened. "Ah yes," nodded the women in the bathhouse. "Despair has rubbed off on Flora Ratoryan like nettles on the hands."

Even Fathaneh Delkasht, whose house adjoined that of the Ratoryans, whose ear was always pressed to the wall, and whose mouth blabbed all over the village, said that Flora was blinding her black eyes with weeping. Her bold glance, which had lusted after all the sweets in the market and aroused the lust of all its traders, was now sunk between her fat heavy eyelids and sulked behind a belly containing a baby whose father was lost.

"I shall tear out my eyes, beloved, *azizam*...I shall tear out my eyes, for their light to shine only in your heart..." Flora began to sing the song she had learned from her aunts and her paternal great-aunts, who flocked in from the neighboring villages to advise her how to bring her little traitor of a husband back home. In their aged hands, speckled with brown patches like spotted cats, they shuffled cards like magicians, upturned coffee cups, and solemnly studied the convolutions of her fate. They instructed Flora to pass her first water of the day, the thickest and strongest tea-colored pee, on a hen's egg that had been laid at dawn, then break the pissed-on egg under a blossoming tree. In the evening she was to burn crackling espand seeds on a censer, fill her innards with their smoke, and plead with the moon to remove the curse that it had laid on her.

Sabiya Mansour, the grandest and severest of the aunts, being the eldest of her father's daughters and able to read the zodiac signs, which made her opinion a final verdict, said that for the burnt espand seeds to achieve their purpose Flora had to yawn profusely and deeply, filling her lungs.

"The more you yawn, child," Sabiya said, and a hush fell on all the aunts, "the more the rascal will dream horrible dreams, his strength will fail him, and he won't be able to get into the holes of the whores that he takes into his stinking bed, his soul will know no rest, and the image of your lovely face will haunt him wherever he goes, everywhere, my poor child."

In addition to the pee and the yawns, Flora was also made to sing the sad song that had been composed especially for such troubles of the heart. The old women drew their cracked lips into the dark caverns of their mouths and agreed with Sabiya Mansour that even husbands who sailed beyond the Caspian Sea to the end of the world could hear this song plainly, and the sadness of its bitter melody brought them back to their wives. That was the song that Gulistan had sung to her lover Horshid, the women chorused squeakily, their eyes moist, their souls yearning, and their flesh astir.

Gulistan was the beloved of Horshid, the royal sculptor. He had carved her form in snowy, purple-veined marble, like her skin, and set it in the middle of a gushing fountain in the palace court. When Horshid heard that Gulistan had been betrothed to the son of Reza Shah, he thrust the heavy chisel into his forehead and died. The following day Gulistan found his body floating in the palace fountain, the goldfish swimming in the caverns of his ears. But when she sang him this song and told him that the story of her betrothal was a lie spread by the prince to alienate her sculptor lover, Horshid revived and the fracture in his skull healed immediately with a fine purple scar.

Enchanted by the ancient legend, and believing wholeheartedly in the power of the song to restore the vanished Shahin to her sweet bosom, Flora hauled her heavy body to the roof of her parents' house, spread a straw mat under the laundry line, taut as the dome of the heaven, chased the birds skyward, and sang Gulistan's song loudly and devoutly from dawn to dusk. In the first days her voice was full of passion that echoed through the rusty rain gutter, and all the villagers coming and going below the Ratoryans' roof paused to wonder about giggly Flora's cries and to mock her longings. Some raised their heads from the alley, shaded their eyes with their hands against the fierce sun, and scolded her for disgracing the village and perplexing the young children with her desire for her husband. Flora did not answer them, only raised her voice till it squeaked, fixed her sad eyes on the distant horizon, and with the hanging wash stroking her hair, aimed her song straight at the hairy passages of her husband's ears.

Finally even the sanctimonious stopped coming to the almond tree alley to shout and warn and order her with a threatening forefinger to come down at once at the command of rabbi *mullah* Netanel the widower. The women, too, stopped coming with their infants hanging from their breasts to pity her for her hard love. Only the gentile children came in gangs to throw pebbles and plum stones at the rutting Flora. "There she is, Flora! Flora! Flora the whora! The whora!" they would sing, clutching their as-yet-hairless bellies and chortling like mice. And Flora would sing and cry, sing and cry, and the rain gutter echoed her tremulously.

Only when her voice had grown hoarse and all but vanished, and the neighbors complained to her abashed parents about the noise she was making, and threatened to throw her from the roof into the garden, did Flora agree to come down and lament in the sooty kitchen. Raising her chin up to the chimney opening, spreading the rolls of her fat neck, she would send her roughened smoky song to the clouds. Flora never doubted for a moment that Shahin would soon return, captured by the melody until its words pierced his ears: "... On the wings of the wind, beloved, I shall sail to you. I shall tear out my eyes, beloved, *azizam*, for their light to shine in your heart alone. My long tresses I shall cut, fill a pillow with them to place under your head. With the dust I shall scrape from your feet I shall paint my eyelids, beloved, *azizam*..."

CHAPTER TWO

FLORA WAS HEAD AND NECK taller than Nazie, and in the cold nights before Flora got married, they would fall asleep in one bed to keep warm. They would tickle each other with their feet, and Nazie would tuck her head between Flora's breasts and pray that she, too, would have such big round ones. Flora's loving body, and the sweetness of her fingers, which toyed with the black down on her back, until the tiny hairs stood on end with delight, protected orphaned Nazie from her awe of the handsome face of her aunt Miriam Hanoum, Flora's mother.

Like all the females on her mother's side, Flora was as healthy as a man and as spoiled as a baby. She got her first period at the age of eleven, and thereafter it appeared at precise intervals as a few scant drops. However, the women of the family were known not only for their robust health, but also for their burnt saucepans and scrawny hens, and like them Flora, too, was lazy and married late.

Homa, her lame older sister, married badly when she was fifteen, by which time it was already said about her that she should be pickled in vinegar water together with cabbages and carrots. Her groom was thin and feeble-minded, still tied to the apron strings of his mother, Mahatab Hanoum, the village singer. She came with him from the far end of the almond tree alley to seek Flora's hand but had to settle for the coarse paw of her sister.

For that matter, Miriam Hanoun, their mother, had been in no hurry to leave her apiculturist parents' house, over which spread golden fans of bees, hovering and buzzing against the sky. She exchanged her father's honeyed comforts and the slothful pleasures she had learned from her mother for her mother-in-law's black kitchen when she was fourteen, only after she had all but driven her bee-keeper father's soul out of his sweet body. For six months her father slaughtered chickens at the entrance to the synagogue, and their pale blood clotted into a thick black paste on the threshold. Though the blood blended with the mud and stuck to their thin soles, the village poor rejoiced in Miriam Hanoum's prolonged spinsterhood, but they, too, eventually agreed that it was time the girl was married, perhaps because they had grown tired of chicken dishes and were hoping that the wedding feast would be varied with the flesh of cattle.

Following her father's frequent visits to the poultry shop, Miriam Hanoum ended up marrying the son of the vendor of fowls, and their wedding guests ate the flesh of geese in honey and black plums, and turkey chicks stuffed with herbs. Peering over the drumsticks, which they tore with their teeth, and the thick gravy, which dripped on their robes, only a few of the villagers noticed what Miriam Hanoum did under the wedding canopy, and their full mouths gaped with amazement. They remembered the proud excited look on the chicken vendor's son's face after he crushed the wineglass underfoot, and then, they said, Miriam Hanoum stamped with her heel on his polished shoe and the glass fragments crunched once more, proclaiming her dominance in her husband's house.

Her husband and his twin brother inherited their father's poultry shop and the two houses in the almond tree alley. Miriam Hanoum bore him three children who suffocated and died at birth and three who breathed and grew up, and then could not be bothered to bear any more. She put Manijoun, her crazy widowed mother-in-law who refused to die, in a small wicker basket that fitted her snugly, and stuck her in a corner of the parlor of the house that had once been her domain. Whenever Manijoun managed to escape from the basket, her trembling legs were so far apart and her knees so low that she seemed to be dancing as she walked. But in the end she got used to the basket and sat in it, braiding her yellowish-white hair, the color of corn silk, into childish pigtails, and made no attempt to leave it until the day she died.

The utter failure of the women of the family at housekeeping was established when Miriam Hanoum was nicknamed by the village women *gorbeh kesafat*—the filthy she-cat. They said that she was the dirtiest housewife in Omerijan, that she was even dirtier than her late mother, a native of Tabriz, a city notorious for its sluttish women, that she was even dirtier than the Shiite women, who, it is said, do not distinguish between lentils and brown beetles, and cook the lot in a single pan with rice and chopped dill. The insects marched in troops into Miriam Hanoum's neglected house, creeping in under the door, flying in through the windows, whole swarms invading it through the gaps in the doorframes and walls, seeking out food that had been forgotten and turned sour, rotten, and stinking.

In the first year of Miriam Hanoum's marriage, Manijoun's mind was still wavering, and she would look at her son from her basket. She gazed at him with scorn when he meekly swallowed the burnt and tasteless meat his wife dumped on his plate, with sorrow when he fled from the stench of her kitchen to the elusive honey scent of her body, and with rage when she heard the china dishes falling from her hands and smashing. And although he pretended to be unaware of his wife's sluttishness and the broken fragments hidden in the bean shed, his mother saw him secretly removing the shards and selling them to the glass peddler for a few pennies. She sent messengers to his aunts, who came one by one from the nearby villages, led by the eldest, Sabiya Mansour, who also lived in Omerijan. Miriam Hanoum's sisters-in-law, too, who had heard the horror stories about the wormy rice and the halva shrouded in gray webs, also hurried over, mincing as they walked. They all tried to teach Miriam Hanoum the skills of a housewife and volunteered to beat her on behalf of her weak husband and her old mother-in-law. But Miriam Hanoum stayed in bed, did not bother to receive them, and following her mother's counsel, pleaded headaches. She did not even serve them black tea. Finally they grew impatient, tied their hair up in kerchiefs, removed their rings and bracelets and demonstrated how the chores should be done, muttering: "Just like her mother, exactly like her mother, *kesafat,* filthy, God carry her off." Energetic and furious, they polished Miriam Hanoum's house, filled it with mouth-watering odors, and she grew even lazier.

"You saw her slim waist, her pretty backside, her big black eyes, and thought you'd found an ant for your son?

Zakhnabut, you should suffocate, what a misery you've brought down on him. Your daughter-in-law is not a bee-keeper's bee daughter—she's a wasp, like her Tabrizi mother, God spare us," they scolded Manijoun in their Isfahani dialect, which dozy Miriam Hanoum neither understood nor cared to understand, until the old woman burst into tears of sorrow and remorse and curled up in her basket.

It was an incident from her childhood that had turned Miriam Hanoum against wifely striving to please her husband with zealous housework and culinary delights. Until that day Shirin, Miriam Hanoum's thick-armed Tabrizi mother, had labored every morning with her rags, polishing the windows and the floors of her house in preparation for her husband's return from his bee-hunting expeditions. In that far-off evening, when he entered his house, clods of damp mud dropped from his road-crusted shoes, leaving a trail of muck on the stone floor that reflected his image like a crystal mirror.

The man stopped and set down the cloth bundle that contained fleshy wood mushrooms whose tips rose from their caps like nipples from breasts, the two bleeding hyraxes he had carried on his shoulder, and the chest of humming bees, in whose furry bodies was stored the rare nectar of the flowering rue. The brightness of the windowpanes and the glass dishes delighted him. Shirin and her children heard his heavy footsteps and gathered around him gaily.

Miriam Hanoum was five years old when she saw her mother standing on tiptoe, her black eyes shining at her husband, as though they, too, had been burnished for hours with the iron-bristle brush. The father, with the children hanging chirpily from his legs and shoulders, stood and stared at his wife. Then he hawked up from his throat a gob of thick phlegm, filled his mouth, and squirted it in the mother's face. Great was the humiliation in the eyes she lowered to the cracks between the floor tiles. Shirin wiped the yellow phlegm from her face with the end of her sleeve and asked her husband tremulously what she had done wrong.

"I had to get it out," he told her. "And the house is so clean and beautiful, I didn't want to soil it. Then you came in and I saw your dirty face, and your dry white hair, and the rags you wear, and I was glad that you'd left me one place to spit on."

From that day on Shirin's spirits fell, and in her sorrow she neglected the chores of the house, which gradually took on a coating of grease, black as an Armenian mourning dress. The rugs stank of the urine of the children, who crawled on them and ate the insects they found in the wall cracks. She was beaten by her husband throughout her life, and she inculcated in her daughters the vanity and idleness that keep the wrinkles away, and in this way the sturdy girls of her family acquired their lazy natures.

But the shine returned to the red copper skillets that Miriam Hanoum had brought as her dowry from her parents' house, and the beetles ceased to swarm in the house in the almond tree alley, because its smell improved. This happened shortly after her husband's twin brother and his wife, Mahasti, died of food poisoning, vomiting black blood. During the seven days of mourning Miriam Hanoum saw how hardworking their little daughter Nazie was, and willingly acceded to her husband's plea to raise the orphaned girl in their home, on one condition only, that she should call her by the respectful title *ameh bozorg,* great-aunt.

CHAPTER THREE

The skin on the faces of Miriam Hanoum and her daughters was as taut as the animal skin on a tambourine frame. Their black eyebrows were as thick and wild as a young man's hair and, when plucked, revealed a grayish forest of needle pricks. There were no deep fissures like knife cuts in the soles of their feet, as in the rock-hard soles of the village women, who walked barefoot, letting the dust of the roads and plantations settle in their cracked flesh. Nor did swollen veins run down their thighs like mountain streams.

Miriam Hanoum had learned from her mother Shirin to neglect the house and pamper the body. When her children were still in her womb, she took pains with their skin and its odor. She ate citrons, rubbed her belly with powdered myrtle and jasmine oil, and nibbled cinnamon sticks. After they were born, she tucked aromatic cloves in their armpits and in their fat creases, and once a week until they were grown she would smear their bodies with spring-flower honey, which is famous for its fragrance. The children would hide in their room for fear of the bees and lick their sticky skin with their little tongues. In the evening

Miriam Hanoum would bathe them in boiled water, rubbing their limbs with date fibers until they shrieked with pain, and then spread soothing beeswax on their skin. Their cheeks reddened, their weight increased, their sweat smelled sweet. When Shahin Bozidozi left Omerijan, that was the smell he took from the folds of Flora's skin and carried in his wanderings.

About Miriam Hanoum it was said that young men fainted on her wedding night. It was said that even after she had borne Homa and Moussa, and was already carrying Flora in her belly, she was still receiving delayed love letters from lads threatening to commit suicide if she dared to marry another.

Her daughters were also famous for their beauty. Before Homa fell from the roof and grew the hump on her back that drew mockery in the alleys, the gentile boys would run after her, forelocks flying, paste a loud kiss on her cheek, and run away crowing with delight. And when Flora passed by the sesame-oil press of the brothers Nasser and Mansour, the two would come out, their black hair glossy, and dance around her with tiny steps and hungry eyes, cooing like demented pigeons: "*Baha, Baha, mashallah,* what a beauty, come to me, *azizam* Flora, come to me…"

Miriam Hanoum's house stood between the house of Fathaneh Delkasht and that of Fathaneh's sister Sultana Zafarollah. Fathaneh and Sultana would both peer from their roofs into the Ratoryan house, and their eyes would meet, grinning. When they sent their children to climb on the windows and spy into their neighbor's yard, or when they climbed on chests and cooking pots to get a view of it, Miriam Hanoum would throw things at them and wish them blind. She believed it was only their evil eyes that had caused Homa to fall off the roof and Flora to be unlucky in her marriage. These witches have been studying the curves of my daughters' breasts since they were olive-sized, she said to Nazie, and in the end the crows will peck out their eyes.

"The day will come," she warned, "when Sultana and Fathaneh will crumble a rock with their envious eyes, the foundation of our house will collapse, and their ceilings will fall down, too, may God carry them off, and then we shall all die."

Sultana Zafarollah's husband flew carrier pigeons from the chimneys on his roof, while on the paving stones of Fathaneh Delkasht's garden yard strutted peacocks with staring eyes in their fans. Her husband sold their flesh to gentiles in the village and their feathers to gentiles overseas. Like the peacocks, Fathaneh walked about the village in colorful Bokhara gowns, waggling her backside like an outspread fan. Over the almond tree alley hovered the peacock feathers of the Delkasht family, the Zafarollahs' pigeon feathers, and the feathers of the geese and chickens that Miriam Hanoum's husband sold in his butcher shop and that she used to stuff pillows and quilts.

In their youth the sisters on either side of the low stone walls were friendly to her and let their children mingle with hers, like the feathers in the wind. Fathaneh fed the peacocks their mixed grain, her sister watered the pigeons, and Miriam Hanoum emptied her feather-filled sacks into a steaming pot under the almond trees. The heavier feathers would sink to the bottom, and the fine goose down floated to the top. When one of the women was unclean, her neighbors would do the cooking for her, even taking special care with the dishes, so that the diners would say that her hands were blessed and note how separate her rice grains were and how succulent the meat. And when one of them carried a heavy burden, the others would say, "Here, love, let me help you, *mashallah,* by night he climbs on your belly and now you have to carry this on your back," and they would all laugh.

In sunshine and in wind the almond alley hummed with women giggling wildly behind their hands, their gowns crumpled and sooty, whining naked infants perched on their tilted pelvis as on a baby seat. They wiped the children's runny noses with their headkerchiefs, and the cooking grease from their fingers with the chadors. Over the cackling of the fowls and the shrieks of the children, the neighbors also chatted with Mahasti, Miriam Hanoum's sister-in-law, Nazie's mother, whose house stood across the alley, and into which Homa and her husband moved when it fell empty. But as the children multiplied like the chicks in the alley, and Miriam Hanoum's daughters grew and matured, envy and the overcrowding drove the neighbors apart, and their bitter hate infected the cooking smells.

Together with the other village women, Fathaneh and Sultana sang mocking rhymes about Miriam Hanoum, laughing into the palms of their hands, but secretly they envied her Flora's beauty. "That one, if she lost one night's sleep from worry, would turn from a ripe fig bursting with honey into a hard dry one," they would say. They were especially provoked by the perfect menstruation of the Ratoryan females, whose sharp odor filled the alley and made people dizzy. They counted the days of the discharge admiringly and would secretly burn myrtle twigs and stand on tiptoe over the flames, naked from the waist down, their legs apart, and pray that the smoke penetrating their wombs would make their days of uncleanness as easy, regular, and sharp as those of Miriam Hanoum and her daughters.

About Miriam Hanoum they said that she was too lazy to love her husband and that he had impregnated her in her sleep, while she dreamed that she was sailing on the waves of the Caspian Sea. They said that she had cunningly given him her urine to drink, which made him cleave to her. About Homa they said that she was lucky, because being lame she was too eager for pleasures, and avoided pissing for days on end in order to push her fingers in there and masturbate all night long. They gossiped about Flora, too, and also envied her, but they all enjoyed hearing her rolling laughter and smelling the honey scent of her body. Even Fathaneh Delkasht said to her that her ovaries were small and tough as nuts and, smiling, patted her round belly as if it were a watermelon. Fathaneh's smile always hovered like that of a puzzled, doubt-ridden person, because she was born without lips around her mouth. Lacking the red folds of flesh, Fathaneh seemed to be smiling against her will.

The women's envy drove Miriam Hanoum apart from her neighbors, and she withdrew into her house, proud and fearful, with her collection of curses. She would scoop out the eyes of the chickens her husband sold, preserve them, and set them in bits of beaten silver, which she hung as good-luck charms on her neck and her children's. In this fashion she sought to ward off her neighbors' evil eye: imprisoned in a ring and hanging on the breast, it was less terrifying. But the further she withdrew, the more they gossiped about her. In a place where pride is the worst sin, Miriam Hanoum barricaded herself with her braids wound around her head like a crown. She cast her eyes far over the heads of the women, above their sagging shoulders and lowered brows, and the hen's eye swinging between her breasts pierced their hearts. Homa, too, who lived not far from her, in a mud-brick house across the alley, closed her door behind her and devoted most of her nights and mornings to desperate efforts to conceive. The village women did not pursue her, but only listened closely and relished her moans.

But since her childhood Flora had enjoyed going out of the house and into the alleys and was liked not only by the Jewish women but also by the gentile ones who lived beyond the synagogue. Whenever she passed the window of one of her friends, Flora would drop something and, raising her rump high in the air, would stoop to pick it up. Her nose would peep out between her breasts, sniffing the cooking odors that invaded the street, and her friends would come out and invite her to enter and taste something. Flora would forget her mother's resentment and laugh bashfully, her eyes narrowing to a long thick row of lashes, and the women would take her by the hand and draw her, light as a cotton ball, into the kitchen, sit her down, and offer her sweets and fruit by the bowlful. While licking the skin of a milk pudding, she would tell them what she had dreamed the night before and funny stories she had heard in the street. The women would toil around her, cooking, cleaning, washing, interpreting her dreams, and Flora's sweet laughter, which gurgled higher and higher, always ending in a short pig's snort, eased their labors. When she laughed, the chocolate drop on her throat jiggled and her face glowed like a gold coin. They vied with each other for her visits and tempted her with her favorite dishes and compliments. "*Betterki,* you should burst, *Baha, Baha, mashallah,* how beautiful you are today, Flora," they would wonder aloud, their eyes growing round, and they scooped up fistfuls of sugared peanuts and wrapped them up in the kerchiefs from their heads, to ensure that she would come back to them.

And in the cold season, when snow fell on the village, they would kindle the coals in the brazier sunk in the floor, and spread a woolen blanket over it, for Flora to tuck her feet into. By and by she would fall asleep. And when she woke up, red-cheeked and disheveled, the babies of the house were asleep at her side and the smells of supper billowed through the rooms. Flora would play with the children, feed them and herself with hazelnuts and pieces of coconut, and tell their mothers the remains of the funny gossip she had heard the day before at the neighbors', until darkness fell.

It was in the neighbors' hot smoky kitchen that Flora first heard about her three brothers who suffocated to death in their sleep before she was born. Then Flora's smile, which opened like the front of a woman's dress when she unbuttons to suckle her baby, slowly closed. Then she understood why her mother was alarmed every time an innocent and hungry alley cat slunk through the window into the house, why she ran in terror to her children, why she chased the creature back into the street, though it did them a favor by catching the house mice. That evening, when Fathaneh Delkasht dredged up from the past the sins of Miriam Hanoum's childhood and youth, the memory agitated the furrows on her prematurely wrinkled brow and the old-woman's beard she had given up plucking.

No one knew why Miriam Hanoum nursed such a hatred for the cats who lived off the village garbage. Those who saw her in her childhood cruelly mistreating them thought it was merely childish mischief. Her beekeeper parents scolded her when they found out that she shut cats in barrels of boiling water, causing tortured howls to come from inside, but for once they did not use blows to teach her to desist.

When she was a young girl, it was her second nature to persecute cats. When the animals fled from her on their soft paws, she would chase after them across the roofs to the end of the village, brandishing the heavy pestle for pounding the meat like a sledgehammer. She showed no mercy to her captured victims, but hammered their soft skulls until they smashed and their vertical pupils closed. She would pluck their tails and burn their long whiskers with sulfur until they curled. "*Aoundareh,* poor things," the villagers threatened her, shaking their hands in the air. "The god of the cats will take terrible revenge on you, *aoundareh,* bad girl."

But Miriam Hanoum did not heed their warnings, and when at last she married and bore her first child on a hot night, her arms were scored with scratches left by the claws of dead cats. Exhausted and happy, Miriam Hanoum fell asleep that night. The apple moon, which gazed through the open window on her and the baby sleeping at her side, was full, yellow, and low-hanging. A hate-filled embittered alley cat stretched his lithe body, climbed in through the open window, padded up to the baby, and crouched on top of it, covering its nose and mouth. When the baby stopped breathing, the cat rose quietly and slunk back out through the window. The village cats did the same thing to the next two babies and in their vengefulness did not even bother to unsheathe their sharp claws.

When Miriam Hanoum found the third baby lying lifeless, with cat's hairs in his ear, she uttered a long howl, and all the village cats rubbed their paws on their noses with satisfaction. Miriam Hanoum and her husband returned from the cemetery determined to do all that was necessary to placate the angry god of the cats.

Sabiya Mansour and her sisters labored in the kitchen until the crescent on the mosque's dome pierced the sinking sun, preparing the finest milk and fish dishes known to Persian cooks. They spread a *sofreh,* a white tablecloth, on the Kashani carpet in the living room and on it arranged the dishes for the feast, so ample that it would have satisfied the village poor, who crowded around the house doors until they were driven out of the alley. The windows were opened, the velvet curtains drawn aside, the doors left gaping. They took Manijoun curled up in her basket and went like mourners to the house of the parents of Fathaneh Delkasht and Sultana Zafarollah, to fast and to pray for the curse to be lifted.

Miriam Hanoum was not in her house when all the village cats entered it like honored guests, sprawled on the rugs, gnawed the fish, and lapped the cheese dishes. When the feast was over, they dozed contentedly on the spread mattresses, and when they rose, they mated on the heaped sacks in the kitchen. In the morning Miriam Hanoum returned to the empty house and gathered up the abundant white, yellow, gray, and black fur, which the cats had shed as a mark of forgiveness. She pressed it into a thick ball, put it into a cloth square, and sewed up its edges into a bag. This bag she hung on the gold chain around her neck when she went to her husband to conceive.

"May God forgive me for telling you this, but after your mother paid for her sins and expressed remorse and asked for forgiveness," Fathaneh sighed and gave the pale Flora a bowl full of red cherries and purple berries, "the cats no longer revenged themselves on her, and she bore poor Homa and Moussa and finally you, darling, may you be healthy, only get married, Flora, get married already..." Fathaneh smiled her lipless smile, and Flora, deeply troubled, stuffed her mouth with cherries, which she forgot to stone.

"Get married, Flora, get married already...," Fathaneh Delkasht urged her. She warned Flora that with every day that passed without a husband her red hole was drying up and turning white, until one day its sides would stick together and it would close up and disappear.

Flora rose, the cherries falling from her lap and scattering on the rug, and walking with her legs wide apart as if she had wet her pants, shedding teardrop after teardrop, she went from Fathaneh's house to Homa's, to tell her sister that she would do anything for her if she would only save her quickly, because it was already starting to stick together, the big lips were sticking to the little ones, and it burned, and she felt she could no longer pee. Homa laughed like a grown-up, her wild breasts bouncing and laughing with her. She opened the shutter with her thick hands, stuck her head out and yelled into the alley: "Ma! *Hoy madar!* Come out a minute! You must hear this, come on, open a minute, Ma." Miriam Hanoum's head appeared in the window, bearing its braided crown.

"Flora's crying like an idiot baby, she's walking as if she's got date honey dripping between her legs," Homa shouted, and everyone heard, whether they wanted to or not. "Fathaneh, her eyes should be scooped out with a teaspoon, told her that her hole was going to disappear, you hear, Ma? Come, tell her that no matter how it burns, the hole doesn't close up so easily, eh, Ma?"

Miriam Hanoum did not laugh, she only cursed Fathaneh, wishing that her belly should ache for all eternity, *inshallah,* and slammed the shutter hard, to close it like her neighbor's evil eye. Homa sent Flora and her clogs home, saying she should ask their mother to tell her about Fathaneh Delkasht's bellyache.

For directly after her wedding night Fathaneh had gone about the village wailing that her belly hurt. She wailed like a baby crying for its mother's milk. The tea and lemon infusions that her sister Sultana made her drink did not help, nor did the fasts she imposed on her. Her pains and complaints did not cease. Until one morning Fathaneh laid her head on her sister's neck, wept, and said she would not return to her husband's house any more. Sultana, the elder, who may be wicked and evil but is merciful to her sister, fetched some carrot oil to rub on Fathaneh's belly, hoping it would ease the pain. Fathaneh raised her dress above her waist, and the bottle fell from her astonished sister's hand and the amber-colored oil spread on the carpet. Blue and purple stains spread on Fathaneh's belly like inkblots, the black runnels of hemorrhage spreading as far as the shadows of her heavy breasts.

Since the time of those frightful bellyaches, when she begged her sister to help, Fathaneh had given birth to six children, and neighborly hatred had sprung up between the sisters and Miriam Hanoum, whose intervening house kept their roofs from touching. Fathaneh gave each of her children a first name of its own, but the village women secretly called them all "the belly-button children," and described a woman who complained about imaginary stomachaches as "suffering like Fathaneh Delkasht when she was barren." For one whole week the virgin peacock breeder had tried in vain to impregnate Fathaneh through the navel, which winked at him from her belly like a blind man's eye. Fathaneh would bite her missing lips, and her groom would drive his member with all his might, pushing and shoving it into the navel, wondering about the pleasure that men derive from the exhausting and frustrating effort of begetting children. Only after Fathaneh consulted with her sister and revealed to her husband the hairy orifice between her legs was the riddle solved, and he penetrated it joyfully and Fathaneh conceived.

Usually, Flora returned late from the neighbors' houses, at the time when the village was going to sleep. Her father and brother would be sleeping when she returned, the wooden clogs ready in their hands to beat her with. But her mother couldn't close her eyes from anxiety about her daughter's maidenhood. The benighted Flora would press her ear to the front door, listen to the snores of the household, then take off her clogs and slip cautiously into the darkened rooms, where mosquitoes buzzed hungrily. Giggling with childish excitement, covering her mouth with her hand, she would tiptoe past her grandmother, who lay asleep in the basket like a baby in its cradle, sneak into the girls' room, and curl up on the mattress beside Nazie.

Though tired from the chores of the day, Nazie was easily awakened from her light sleep by her cousin's suppressed giggles. She would open her eyes, observe the black silhouette that filled the room, and play with her under the mosquito net until Flora fell asleep.

After a few minutes Miriam Hanoum would come into the girls' room. The burning wick she carried in one hand and shaded with the other cast flickering shadows on the walls. She would hurry to close the door behind her and kneel exhausted beside her daughter, muttering about honor and shame and cursing the village women, above all Fathaneh and Sultana, upon whom she called down ailments as yet incurable. Her lovely face gleamed with the oiliness of her healthy skin, her eyes shone under the plucked brows, and her regular teeth ground angrily.

First she would make sure that little Nazie was asleep, then she would take the cover off Flora, turn her dress up above her waist, loosen the string that held the cloth pants, and pull them down quickly. It was as though Flora were a baby who had soiled herself and her mother were about to clean her and change her diaper. Under the thin gauze Nazie saw her aunt's fingers swiftly uncovering Flora's long legs, which gleamed white in the darkness. Miriam Hanoum would part the heavy thighs, exposing the black woolly thicket. Flora, her thighs and genitals spread wide, giggled in her sleep.

Miriam Hanoum's hoarse voice ceaselessly addressed her dead father, cursing him for marrying her off against her will, and telling him about the disgrace that Flora caused them, the food she ate in other people's houses, as though there were not enough to eat at home, and again cursed the women of the alley, may their livers burst into flames. The elongated black shadows on the stone wall were restless. While communing with her father's spirit, she pushed two fingers into her daughter's secret part and rolled her eyes to the ceiling.

Through the wavy diaphanous net Nazie saw Miriam Hanoum's face grow serious and attentive, as if listening to a faraway flute playing, while her hands burrowed into the cavern between her daughter's legs. The tallow dripped from the earthen saucer onto the floor, the light of the flame shivered on the ceiling, and the mosquitoes danced madly around it. Sinking deeper into sleep, Flora uttered a little chuckle of pleasure and embarrassment, and promptly received a sharp slap on her cheek and a vicious pinch on her fat soft thigh. The laugh turned to a sob.

Miriam Hanoum kept digging into her half-asleep daughter, searching for gold. When she found it, she froze for a moment and her face softened. Only then did she pull her moist fingers out of the girl's heavy body. Glad to have found the family honor, she also examined attentively Flora's breasts and large waist, searching for marks of bites and sucks. Finally she would dress her again, cover her with the blanket, and go to sleep at her husband's side.

Miriam Hanoum was not the only one who feared the wintry wind that fluttered Flora's skirts, or the honeyed summer sweat that stuck the veil to her breasts, outlining the nipples with big damp patches. The neighboring women, too, in whose houses Flora sprawled on the cushions, spreading her hair on the lace trimmings, were afraid of the young girl's big body. When their husbands came home in the evening Flora's laughter would suddenly lose its charm, and her hostesses would urge her to go home, swearing that they could hear Moussa's white hound barking. They had all learned the bitter lesson of ugly Nosrat, who failed to hide Flora's big body, which seemed to burst its garments, from her husband's eyes, and since then there was neither peace in her house nor love in her heart.

Violating the matchmakers' rule, ugly Nosrat had married a tall handsome man, who wore a heavy mustache and eyeglasses. Like all the women who refuse to take a husband as ugly as their fathers, and succeed in marrying handsome, hairy-faced men, it was Nosrat's fate to live in fear. But God, who had dug all those pits in her skin, had also given her a man's wit.

Every night Nosrat would wait for her husband to start snoring, then leave his bed and go to the well. Under its lid she kept a jar of fresh goats' butter. To guard the flame of her husband's love she would smear a thin layer of butter on the lenses of his glasses, then go back to their room and place them by his side. At daybreak he would put them on and be well pleased with his wife's face. Her complexion glowed as in a dream, her pockmarks vanished, and her nose was shorter. In the evening, by which time the butter had melted away in the midday sun, darkness veiled her ugliness.

One night Nosrat fell asleep before she had spread butter on her husband's eyesight. In her dream she descended to the bottom of the Black Sea, and there she saw strange, blue-faced women rubbing their bare breasts against the rough coral reefs, their fishtails quivering. She woke from the dream as from a nightmare and ran to the well, but in her hurry she dropped the eyeglasses, which smashed on the stone pavement. In the morning, when she returned from the glazier to her husband who was waiting at home for his glasses, she recalled having promised Flora that if she came that day, she would make her a sesame-oil-and-nuts cake.

Flora was then thirteen, generously curved, her hair gathered like the tail of one of Shah Pahlavi's thorough-bred horses, her red dress embroidered with euphorbias. Nosrat's husband met her at the door and saw her through his mended and clean eyeglasses. She looked to him like a necklace of fiery red peppers. His tongue burned, and he put out his hand to pluck one and taste it. Since that day Flora ceased to visit Nosrat, and Nosrat gave up tucking sugar cubes in the thickets of her armpits and putting them in her husband's mouth, for the salty sweat and the sugary sweetness to run together on his tongue.

CHAPTER FOUR

THE BOILED CHICKPEAS, which had been soaking in water since the night before, had softened and shed their transparent skins, revealing their yellow faces and clownlike pointy heads. Nazie pounded them with the heavy pestle in the stone mortar, and every dull thud crushed them more, until they became a soft yellow paste. Then Nazie pounded the chicken pieces, which she had earlier torn apart with her fingers and cooked with dried lemons. The steady pounding of the pestle in the mortar dictated a regular stone-on-stone rhythm to Flora's singing and slowed down Nazie's thoughts.

Then she shook herself, thrust under the pot a few chunks of wood she had gathered that morning, and added the stripped bones of the cooked chicken. In between the bones she put lumps of olive pulp and a smoldering ember she had scooped up with a skillful bare hand from the oven, then she filled her lungs and blew on the flame.

"Nazie, you dope, why are you making so much smoke!" Throttled by the smoke, Flora stopped singing and rubbed her eyes with her fists. "Can't you see what you're doing? You're making me cry. Don't I cry enough without it?"

Nazie did not answer, but her reddened eyes, narrowed by the stinging smoke, shed tears while the fire caught. The flames danced between her tears, and she shaded them with her dirty hands, the fingers with their bitten nails stiff and straight, pushing them closer and closer to the lively, provocative tongues of the cooking fire. Chinks of light shimmered and twinkled through the skin between her fingers. She held her breath until the fire licked her fingertips. Flora, coughing, did not take her eyes off Nazie, and she uttered a little shriek when Nazie pulled her hands back from the fire and quickly put her scorched fingers in her mouth. She sucked them like an infant, and the traces of hummus under her nails dissolved in her mouth.

"Dopey." Flora laughed in alarm, and her smile was like the parting of a heavy curtain. Nazie also laughed, rose on tiptoe, stretching over the oven to open the one little window in the walls of the sweltering kitchen. She pressed her body to the sooty, greasy wall, and her skirt was pulled up by her arms, the hem rising above the thin, childish calves. When her hand reached the window, a grunt of strain broke from her throat and from its hinges, and it opened. A chilly breeze of an early winter evening blew into the kitchen and made Flora huddle on her swans. The rustling of the shaken almond trees in the alley also entered the girls' hearts. The flame trembled, and the thick smoke rose to heaven.

Nazie in her sad shell did not know where Flora's big laugh bubbled up from into her mouth, did not understand how it was possible for Flora to be beaten murderously all over her body by Moussa, until her cries alarmed the whole village, yet go on laughing till her big eyes narrowed like a Chinese girl's. Even on the eve of Passover the year before, when Moussa could no longer stand her laughter and whipped the leather belt out of his father's Sabbath trousers, Flora went on laughing fearfully and snorting like a piglet. The demons of Omerijan toyed with Moussa's mind, playfully rolled his eyes, yelled through his throat about honor and shame, while the belt in his hand flogged his sister's legs as though it possessed a life of its own. Flora grasped her bruised feet with one hand, while with the other she covered her mouth, to suppress the wild laugh and protect her teeth from the writhing belt.

The furniture and other household objects had invaded the street to be aired, while Nazie labored in the kitchen preparing the holiday feast. For the past week she had scoured and polished the house, and the family ate outdoors, sitting in a circle on a rug in the shade of an almond tree. At the end of the meal they would carefully step into the circle and shake their clothes thoroughly. Nazie was roasting hazelnuts, almonds, and peanuts in the oven and extracting the stones from the soft juicy flesh of dates, when she heard, over Manijoun's demented murmuring, Flora's welling laugh and snorts and the whistling of the belt that flogged her flesh. The sounds led her to the closed bean shed. Nazie tried to open its door, but Moussa was leaning against it with all his strength, and she sent Miriam Hanoum to fetch Homa from her house and her husband from the poultry shop—quickly, because Moussa was killing Flora.

Nazie pounded on the door with her hands, yelling to him to let her in.

"Stop, Moussa, by God, let me in!"

"Don't you come in, Nazie, go away right now, don't come in," his voice shook through the door.

"Come, Nazie, please come, he's killing me," laughed Flora.

Outside, Moussa's hound barked as if he, too, were being chastised by a demon, and the door finally gave under Nazie's blows. The closed shed contained Flora's dowry—bedding and sheets in wicker baskets, copper dishes and crystal platters for Passover, garments for winter and summer—as well as dried foodstuffs, roasted fruits and pickled vegetables, liquors in glass bottles clad in woven straw, and tins full of opium to be smoked for pleasure and to ease Moussa's painful breathing, for he had suffered from asthma since childhood. Flora was squeezed between a wooden barrel filled with cabbages pickled in salt and a loose bag, half full of brown lentils. She had torn it with her fingernails, and the lentils had scattered all over the shed floor, like insects come to nibble the foodstuffs. Her feet, which were tied together like the legs of a rebellious fluttering hen, were bleeding. To make her pain worse, Moussa had sprinkled on them coarse salt crystals he had taken from one of the sacks. Flora was close to fainting, and still her hair was trapped between his fingers.

"*Aoundareh,* mercy, Moussa, *aoundareh…*" Nazie thrust her little body between him and Flora and hugged him with both arms. She pressed her head to his belly, and the stink of the butcher-shop carcasses filled her nose. Sweat dripped from Moussa's face, which glowed with a strange light, and his adolescent pimples burned in his cheeks. Above his coal-black, narrowed eyes his even blacker brows met in a single dense hairy line. His ears and nostrils were as red as Flora's legs, and fresh scratches showed on the plum skin of his neck. His breathing was noisy and shallow, like his dog's grunts, and saliva ran from the corners of his open mouth.

"So you're not laughing any more? Ah?" Moussa yelled, drawing away from them both and moving to the corner of the shed, all his teeth showing. "So help me, *inshallah,* if I don't take you to the synagogue tomorrow, when everybody comes for the prayer of the three pilgrimages. I'll take your right leg and tie it to this gatepost of the synagogue, then your left leg, see? Ah?" He turned to his parents and Sabiya Mansour, who arrived in a panic at the shed, while the mice fled in panic between their legs toward the alley. "And tomorrow morning all of Omerijan will come with the women and children and pass under the synagogue gate to look at my sister's hole and see that she's a virgin. A virgin! A virgin! Then they won't say that the Ratoryan girls run around the village like hungry she-cats, they won't say that, ah? They won't say that Flora's brain and her hole are playing backgammon together, ah? I swear by this holy festival, I swear, if I don't do this thing, ah? I'm a dog, myself, I am, if I don't do this to you, ah? God carry you off…"

He did not stop talking until Nazie returned with a copper bowl filled with water and a handful of jasmine flowers in her hand, to soothe his coughing and his shaken lungs. He wiped the spit from the corners of his mouth and drank the water in one go. Fresh drops ran from his lips, but the grimace of rage did not leave his face. When he had calmed down, Nazie brought a glass for Miriam Hanoum, who had turned pale, and one for her husband, who stood in the door of the shed, his trousers hitched up above his waist and his butcher's apron soiled with blood.

Sabiya Mansour crossed her arms on her breasts, shook her head, and clicked her tongue.

Outside, Moussa's dog had ceased to howl and the neighboring women, who had gathered at the door with their children, scattered to tell the villagers what had transpired in the Ratoryan household. In the silence that fell, the only sounds were the lentils falling one by one from the torn sack, and the screams of Manijoun from her basket, begging God to take her at last.

During the *Seder*, Moussa again beat Flora when they all hit one another with the scallions and leeks and sang *Dayenu*. The strong odors made her eyes sting till her tears ran, at long last, and Moussa was triumphant. But the next morning Flora's legs were not spread on the synagogue gate, nor by night when she slept, because from Passover Eve until the end of Shavuot she neither left the house nor saw a single stranger. When Miriam Hanoum wanted to go shopping, her husband would leave Moussa in charge of the poultry shop and hurry home to guard his daughter. Or else Homa was summoned to guard her sister, and when their mother returned, she would find them quarreling as they used to do in their childhood, and Flora's skin was all red from pinching. Flora was not even allowed to go to the privy on her own. Nazie was sent to accompany her and supported her when she limped on her wounded feet.

To neighbors who asked about her, Moussa and his father replied that Flora was very ill. But no one believed them, because Fathaneh and Sultana had talked about the screams in the bean shed, and the Ratoryan females were known for their good health. The village women tried to visit her. Bearing in their hands their young friend's favorite pastries and sweets, they knocked on the door with the iron knocker shaped like a roaring lion and peered curiously and longingly around Miriam Hanoum, who blocked the entrance with her body. After they left, Miriam Hanoum would rest her back against the door, shutting her eyes tight and cursing them that on the happiest day of their lives they would suffer from toothache.

But in the end everyone believed that Flora was ill, even Fathaneh and Sultana. They said that the girl was yellow and thin like the moon at the end of the month. They said that she had an infection of the kidneys, because her mother, the filthy she-cat, had neglected the house and her children's health, and that she should be treated with the smoke of goats' droppings. And Fathaneh Delkasht told everyone that she had glimpsed Flora from the roof, and she had permanent pockmarks, her lips had dried and roughened, their color had faded, and she could no longer part them to laugh as before. Her sister Sultana added that her period came only once in three months, in the form of black clots, causing her much pain, and all the women grinned with satisfaction.

Nazie shook herself again and cut a piece from the *dombeh,* the solid chunk of sheep fat, which was kept above the cool water-well. The *dombeh* was stripped by the sheep peddler from between the hind legs of a mature ewe. The lump of fat, which dangled like udders when she followed his flute, was pulled off without protest. Nazie melted the rancid piece in a pot, and its sharp smell spread through the house. Shallots glazed slowly in the hissing fat. Now Nazie compressed the chickpeas-and-chicken paste into balls, pushed them into the rice, and placed the lid on the pot. Even before Moussa and his father closed the poultry shop and returned home hungry, to see what Nazie had done with the feathered hen they had sent her wrapped in brown paper, she had also quickly baked on the back of an upturned copper frying pan the *labash,* the thin dry wafery bread. But as soon as she had turned the dough over and browned it on the other side, Flora dragged her to the roof, which tempted the eyes and ears to penetrate the neighbors' yards, because she heard from afar a woman's cry sounding like a dying wail.

CHAPTER FIVE

Although he was short and stubborn, Shahin Bozidozi was not an especially talented cloth merchant. He had learned the art of trading from his father, whose legs were even stumpier than his. When Shahin was five years old, his father pushed his mother into the mouth of the burning oven. From that time on, the son accompanied his father on his business travels and learned how to sell cheap linen cloth for the price of silk.

On the day she died, Shahin's mother had been baking bread with floured hands. She hummed old love songs to her son, who was sitting in the kitchen with her. When the father returned home, he pressed his ear to the door to listen to her singing and was overcome by jealousy. Suspecting that she was humming those wistful songs because she had fallen in love with another man, and perhaps had even betrayed him, he threw her into the flames, and Shahin was left orphaned and hungry for his mother's bread.

Shahin spread on the back of his father's stolen donkey a large bag of Arab cloth, embroidered with owls for good luck in their business. The father smeared avocado pulp on his son's face, to protect his young skin from the sun of the roads, and they set out together. They tied the bolts of cloth to the owl bag, and on the donkey's neck they hung a nosebag full of fodder, so that it could feed at will, and as they walked, the bag and the rolls of cloth swung from side to side. Shahin led the way, pulling on the donkey's neck with a strong palm-fiber rope, while the widowed father ambled behind the animal's tail, green in the face, dreaming about a silkworm breeding plant that he planned to set up some day, his head full of butterflies and money.

When his father died, Shahin inherited his dream of silk butterflies and the stolen donkey, a few tricks of the trade, and the shameful surname Bozidozi, goat stealer. Shahin buried his father in their town Babol, by the side of his mother, mounted the donkey, and set out to wander all over the country, whose outline resembled a startled cat, with its ears pricked and its back arched. On the first evening of his travels the towering clouds in the sky hung so low, so heavy and black, that Shahin thought they were about to collapse on Persia and crush it. A thin yellow streak of light separated heaven and earth. When the strip of sunlight vanished behind the clouds and the sky became completely black and blended with the earth, a frightful storm burst out of the darkness. Tremendous rolls of thunder beat giant drums, and a satanic bolt of lightning hit the donkey's tail. The terrified beast howled, flung Shahin off its back, and fell down, dead as a lump of coal, beside him.

Shahin rose, scraped the mud off his robe, and continued his journey to Tehran on foot, shaken, as anyone would be if the angel of death had tapped him on the nape and then vanished. He stuck the scissors like a dagger into his cummerbund and carried the colorful bolts of cloth, soiled with the dust of the road, in his arms, struggling against the powerful wind that blew on them and caused them to flutter like banners.

In Tehran he stole a new donkey, a foal whose white belly matched the patches around its eyes, to be his surrogate in the next thunderstorm. En route to Isfahan, which lies in the Persian cat's navel, he also picked up a Muslim apprentice, a tender young lad whose pupils were as small as pinheads. On stormy nights, when the dreaded silvery lightning that was intended for Shahin flickered over his head, the apprentice would hold his hand and stroke it, and on hot summer nights his little mustache tickled his master's neck when he kissed him.

The apprentice knew how to lead him to the wealthiest and vainest Shiite ladies in every town and village they passed, and Shahin repaid him generously. First the apprentice would point to a handsome stone house surrounded by a low wall of sunbaked bricks, and smile. Then the two would seek a suitable hiding place nearby, unload the donkey, and spread the embroidered owls on the ground. The apprentice would turn on the little tap of the tea urn, which was full of plum liquor, pour some into his glass, and blow on it, as if it were hot tea. While the apprentice sipped the liquor, Shahin smoked opium in his long-stemmed pipe. When they finished drinking and smoking, the apprentice would turn his back to Shahin and his face to the east, so that the first light would fall on his eyes, and they would fall asleep, entwined together.

When the sun rose and the sky over Persia turned blue, Shahin and his apprentice would watch the householder and his sons emerging from their house into the street.

Shahin would smooth his unkempt eyebrows with spit-moistened little fingers, then spit right and left for luck, and order the apprentice to stack the bolts on his out-stretched hands and tuck them under his arms. Finally the lad was to bang on the door with the knocker and then make himself scarce.

Whenever Shahin employed the sales method his father had taught him, tears of respect would rise in his eyes. His weak eye would flutter like a butterfly, and the good one squinted excitedly in sympathy. When he stood on the threshold, his smile gleaming like oil and his eyebrows moist and combed, he would hear his father's voice crowing: "The worm always longs for its cocoon, you clot!" In his lifetime, this triumphant cry sealed every successful deal he brought off.

Like him, Shahin would be invited to enter, laden with his bright materials. He was met by the sour odors of sleep and the yogurt that had been eaten for breakfast hanging in the rooms and exhaled by the housewife's mouth. Shahin would imitate his father's broad gestures and his mincing steps as he unrolled the bolts like great rivers on the floor. And before the yawning housewife could protest, the entire room was flooded with varicolored textiles, and Shahin had launched into stories about his wanderings in China, whence he had brought his fine merchandise. The housewife's imagination sailed with him, and the flapping fabrics blew a soft, seductive breeze into her disheveled hair. When at last she chose the material she liked best, Shahin would compliment her, saying that its hue and texture suited her well, and flatter her at length about her beauty and good taste, even if her complexion was shriveled and greenish and marred by pockmarks. Then he would begin to measure.

He would take the goatskin tape and measure the housewife's length and breadth, around her waist and bust, his squinting eye skimming hungrily and nervously over her body. Some women gave in to him at once while he was measuring their curves, flattering their big bosom, or pressing against their back, rubbing his member against the warm backside. Others succumbed to him and his artificial silk later, when he cut with infinite care the material they had chosen for their new dress, and to show them how good it was and pleasant to the touch, he would pass it over their throat, press it firmly to the nipples till they stiffened, or rub it skillfully between their legs.

Another important rule he had learned early from his father was never to insert the worm that hung between his legs into the cocoons of alien women, lest gentile butterflies issued from them. Faithful to the vow he had made to his father, Shahin always kept a small silk square handy, for dumping his seed and wiping his member.

Afterward Shahin would retie his trousers, put on his cloak, and roll up the fabrics, which had been wrinkled by the bodies' movements and stained with their sweat. He would leave the vain housewife the length of material free of charge, pat her flesh, and praise its ample charms. The housewife, doubly delighted with her good fortune, and certain that she would never again set eyes on the Babolian peddler who had seduced her, would begin to plan the new dress she would make from the gift of silk. After thanking him and wishing him a safe journey, she would provision him with bread and pastries and all but push him out of her house before her children, who were running around naked outside, should see him.

But that evening, when the memory of Shahin's body had almost faded from her heart, he would show up again on her doorstep, his squinting eye spinning around and a merchant's smile spread on his face.

"Eh…Good evening, *shaab khair,* sir, good evening, ma'am…," he would say politely, lowering his glance humbly to avoid the eyes of the blanching woman and the astonished man.

"*Bebakhshid,* forgive me, honored sir, for disturbing you at this late hour. Allow me to ask you, sir, has your honored wife already shown you the material I cut for her this morning? Did you like the color and the embroidered pattern? If you wouldn't mind, could you pay me now? I am a hungry itinerant and have not eaten since yesterday, and I wish to proceed on my long and difficult journey."

And while the husband shouted at his wife for wasting his money and frittering it on clothes, cosmetics, and jewelry, and she swore that it was the last time and begged him tearfully to pay the merchant the excessive amount he demanded, only get the rascal out of their house, Shahin rested his back against the doorjamb and toyed with the little silk bag that the seed of Baboli cloth merchants had stiffened since the morning. When at last he returned to his donkey with the triple price he had extracted from the gentile woman's husband, his blinking eyes would again water with admiration for his late father, who had raised him on his own from childhood and bequeathed him a way in the world.

"The cocoon always longs for its worm, you clot!" he would shout triumphantly at his apprentice, and whip the donkey's hindquarters to stir him up and make him bray.

But the father's business method did not always work.

Some women drove him out of their houses with shouts and blows for his impudent fingers. There were also some days of pleasure at the end of which Shahin was left with neither the cloth nor the money—only his little seed bag to toss in his hands, every limb in his small body beaten and sore, because he had fallen between the legs of a woman whose husband was jealous, miserly, and strong.

In the third month of the spring, a little before the feast of Shavuot, Shahin reached the village of Omerijan in the foothills of the Alborz range. The money he had made selling the scarlet cloth of the prince's cape was almost gone, and he was badly bruised because of an unfortunate incident, following which he resolved to give his paternal heritage a rest. He had succeeded in seducing an old spinster of seventeen with a length of red silk that he tied around her bare hips, saying, "Shake it." Her father, who was sleeping in the next room, was awakened by the rustle of the artificial silk, and when he saw his naked daughter waggling her hips and bleeding between her legs, he beat Shahin repeatedly and at length, until the anxious apprentice broke into the house, carried his master in his arms out into the street, and saved his life. When he married Flora Ratoryan, Shahin's right arm was still encased in a plaster containing egg yolks and cumin, and his good eye looked as if painted with kohl. On their wedding night Flora discovered a long-winged grasshopper tattooed over his tailbone.

Shahin Bozidozi and his apprentice rode in on their donkey through the *darvazeh moshtari,* the wide itinerants' gate in the northern side of the dentated village wall, through which the merchant caravans came and went. They left through the southern gate, *darvazeh jaudan,* close to the crowded Jewish quarter, the Jubareh. Through the eastern, solar, gate the sun shone and entered the village every day, as later did the moon.

When they entered the village, Shahin seized the donkey's ears and his apprentice clasped him from behind, clutching his cummerbund and embracing his waist. No sooner did they pass through the gate than they were hit by the stench of the village, their breath grew short, and a dizzy spell made them lose their balance and fall with the bolts of cloth off the stumbling donkey's back. Shoulder to shoulder, they stood on the southern side of the village and pissed into the canal at the foot of the wall, into the water that flowed, chill and turbid, down from the snowy mountaintops. The sweet scent of the flowering almond trees filled their nostrils. The dense almond copse enveloped the Jews' neighborhood, screening it from the other quarters as its alleys wound among the trees. It did not protect the inhabitants like the fortified stone wall that surrounded the Armenian quarter, but in the spring the fragrance of its blossoming trees overcame all the village stinks and enveloped the Jubareh like a cloud.

Flora and Shahin met on that morning of dizziness and headache. Shahin, who had resolved to abandon temporarily his father's method of selling fabrics, planned to dispose of his remaining bolts by more conventional practices. When he knocked on the Ratoryan door, neither spitting first for luck nor grooming his eyebrows with spit, Flora's mother invited him into the house to show her the materials stacked up on his outstretched arms, with only his forehead and thinning hair showing above them. Despite the injunction of her husband and son not to let anyone into the house, and allow no stranger's eye to glimpse the body of the captive Flora, the vain Miriam Hanoum could not resist the temptation. She only poked her head quickly into the street, to make sure that the tattletales did not see whom she was pulling into her house, but all she saw out there were the dizzy donkey and apprentice, bathed in the spring sunlight.

"Quick, quick, come in, come in, *vavaila,* before my husband shows up and sees you here...," she said and closed the low door behind them. Shahin stumbled slowly into the house, scratched his sun-freckled, fungus-infected bald patch, and grinned uncomfortably. He found it hard to believe that the fame of his amorous exploits had spread so far among the women, covered the distances as he did, and wandered from village to village, until they waited for him in the morning, in possession of the house, urging him to untie the colored threads of his trousers string. But although he had sworn always to follow in his father's ways, Shahin had promised himself and his apprentice to abstain for a while, at least until his bones knit and his bruises faded.

"But see, lady, I don't do those jobs any more...no no, *nah nah,* if you want to buy...me, I...," he said and fingered his broken arm sadly, recalling the pain his trade had cost him. He was relieved when he realized that Miriam Hanoum had never heard about his package deals, though the pride of his awakening loins was slightly hurt. Unfamiliar with normal methods of salesmanship, and not knowing what to do without his voyager's tales and nimble fingerwork, he stood on the Kashani carpet as thoughtful and unsure as a tyro. But Miriam Hanoum, fearful that her husband or son might arrive suddenly and raise hell because Flora's punishment was violated, commanded him to spread the materials before her, and he followed her orders obediently and in silence.

While she greedily felt the fabrics and stroked her cheeks with them, Shahin stood in a corner of the room, smelling the hot peppers that were being fried in the kitchen together with chopped onion seasoned with cumin and turmeric, and looking at wrinkled Manijoun lying curled up in her basket, smiling at him in her sleep like a toothless puppy. It dawned on him that there was more than one woman in the house who would want a new dress for the summer, and more than a single dish for the midday meal.

When Miriam Hanoum ordered him to cut the material she had chosen—a gray one with silver pears woven into it—he restrained himself and did not wrap it in his usual manner over her partly covered breasts. He smelled river fish roasting on charcoal, and when he saw a little girl going out with a knife in her hand to cut vegetables in the garden, he guessed that there would also be a cucumber salad, cabbage, and radishes, and a heap of fresh basil leaves to chew. Then, when Nazie returned from the garden with the white skull of a cabbage, and could not decide between a plain velvet and a floral one, and called Flora to come and help her choose—and Flora emerged from her darkened room, flushed with sleep and laughing to see a stranger in their house—Shahin understood that there was dessert, too, and that it was sweet.

CHAPTER SIX

To MAKE SURE OF THE QUAL-
ity of the match, Miriam Hanoum and her husband went
to Azizolla the fortune-teller, who was also famous as an
expert maker of charms. At first Miriam Hanoum thought
that she could manage without him, because she believed
she had a natural gift for interpreting dreams. She wrote a
dervish charm and went and sat down at the mouth of the
alley leading to the bathhouse, to hear what the passersby
were saying. If they talked about their children, about the
fish they intended to buy in the market, or the heat of the
approaching summer, it would mean that the match was a
good one, and she would not need Azizolla's skills. But the
passersby seemed to make a point of talking about the
death of their loved ones, about their poverty and ailments,
and the terror-stricken Miriam Hanoum, convinced that
misfortune awaited Flora, hurried with her husband to the
fortune-teller's house.

The man sat cross-legged on a rug, whispering a prayer
with his eyes shut. He gestured with his purple-veined
hands to the visitors to come in and sit down before him.
He passed the fingertips of his right hand over the edge of

the closed book of fortunes, moved them up and down like a blind man, and abruptly opened the fateful page that would reveal the quality and future of the match. Then he opened his eyes and studied the text closely, and his face darkened. He remained silent for a long time, his eyebrows arched, as if at the sight of a gloomy future, and the purple veins in his hands turned blue. Miriam Hanoum cursed all her enemies, calling down an earthquake to swallow up their houses, but then Azizolla's face suddenly cleared. He discovered that he was holding the book of fortune upside down.

Having turned it around and leafed through seven pages forward and seven back, and read the text correctly, he hastened to allay all Miriam Hanoum's doubts and anxieties. In exchange for three coins he declared that Flora and Shahin's future would be blessed, and concluded with his usual words of wisdom: "Ten bridegrooms will come to the house, ten bridegrooms will look at the girl through the window, but only one bridegroom will enter and take her to his own house at last. . ."

The bride and groom spent the last three days before the wedding in the sun, he with his eyes shut, and she washing his hair with kerosene to expel the hundreds of head lice that swarmed in it. Once his hair had been rinsed and dried, Shahin rested his backside on the embroidered swan cushion and his head between his future wife's legs, and Flora picked the lice out one by one, baring her teeth with the effort, her fingers proceeding gently from hair to hair. She cracked the kerosene-dazed insects between her fingernails, each sound a tiny knell of crushing and death. Shahin surrendered to the sun and the fingers stroking his scalp, and dozed off between the soft thighs. He also got rid of his intestinal lice, having inserted coarse salt and raw pumpkin seeds into his rectum, and the long white worms came out with his feces.

But Flora's hair was washed by Homa with an infusion of chamomile flowers, to make her curls glossy. To whiten her yellow teeth, she rubbed them back and forth with a green pecan shell, until her gums bled. Homa also made up their eyes with blue henna, which added a bluish cunning to Flora's mischievous eyes, and widened her own like a demon's eyes.

The village hair stripper smeared Flora's legs with a thin layer of melted sugar, stripped the hair off her legs and armpits, where it had grown long and stiff under her clothes, and the thick black pubic hair, which extended to the back of her fat-dimpled thighs and marched uniformly and stubbornly toward the buttocks. The hair stripper was known for her delicate and skillful fingers, but Flora shrieked with pain. Angry that Miriam Hanoum's pampered daughter was giving her a bad name with her shrieks, the woman hurt her on purpose, lacerated her skin, and Flora's screams grew louder.

The woman used tiny iron pincers to pluck the soft hairs that writhed down the spine to the tailbone, branching at the waist in opposing directions, the fine fur clothing its curves. When she began to pluck the strip of fuzz that grew between the breasts and continued like a downy tail over the sweet childish belly, Flora howled like a tortured captive. All the village women cheered her loudly, urging her to be brave. The cheers grew louder still when the hair stripper dipped cotton threads in the melted sugar, wound them like scissors around the thumbs and forefingers of both her hands, and rubbed them up and down to remove Flora's mustache and the fine down that grew under her ears.

Flora saw the woman's eyes bulging with the effort of uprooting all the hairs, determined to leave not a single one. Observing her from kissing distance, she saw her lips squeezed into a circle, the furrows on her upper lip forming a wreath of age, rage, and concentration. Irritably, the woman joined the others' singing, and Flora, breathing in her stale exhalation, was astonished to see that despite her craft, the hair stripper's face was covered with thick masculine bristles—under her nose, on her cheeks, even on her black forehead. She kept thrusting her head forward, like the birds that strutted in the alley, and the flabby flesh of her arms swung like wattles. And when Flora's nose was stuck between the woman's breasts she saw in the recess of her armpit a thicket of curly black hair.

"What will you do when you give birth, Flora? How much will you scream when you give birth?" the hair stripper muttered, uprooting, stripping, and hurting, while gripping Flora's legs between her knees to prevent her from moving or escaping.

Flora's face was red and burning. She could not stand the pain any longer and refused to let the woman strip the down that grew under her other ear. On the eve of her wedding only one of her cheeks was smooth and red, and the other was as hairy as in her spinster days, and all the village women agreed: beautiful like her mother, and just as lazy. But only after she was allowed to pluck the excess hairs from the eyebrows and around the crimson nipples did the hair stripper agree to smear the red henna Flora was longing for. The powder that had been soaked in water and turned into a thick paste with a sharp sweatlike smell was spread thoroughly on the palms of her hands, on her neck, and between her toes. Given a mirror to admire herself in, Flora saw the orange stains blooming on her red skin, and thought they were lovely.

At the end of the seven weeks from Passover, at Shavuot, the wedding was held at Flora's parents' house. The bells rang out in the tower of the village wall, and torches flared in the house wall, attracting guests and moths. The *ketubah* (marriage contract) was decorated with peacocks and imaginary birds, strangely colored and winged, such as had never been seen in the village. The rabbi *mullah* Netanel, who was also a matchmaker and a scribe, had written the *ketubah* in red and silver on parchment paper, with a frame of gilt curlicues.

All the villagers came in droves to see, at long last, the laughing bride, who was wearing flat shoes so as not to embarrass her short husband, and a floating dress of rich white material. Shahin had told her that it was an especially fine and costly fabric, which he himself had imported at great risk from the Atlas Mountains in Morocco. She wore the bridal nose ring, a glittering gold hoop, and silenced the mocking chants of the children, who had stolen out of their beds, their faces sweet and smooth, by sticking her tongue out at them.

When the *thar* and violin players had taken their place on the terrace facing the garden courtyard, and were warming the drumskins by the fire, they received the first glass of arrack, poured from a potbellied, narrow-necked bottle, which contained a yellow citron as big as a man's heart. The citron was a mere bud on a branch in the courtyard, no bigger than a fish's eye, when its life's bottle was carefully slipped over it. The bottle was tied to the branch, and the citron matured inside, after which the spirit kept it from rotting. Having poured the arrack from a height into the copper goblets, raising a rich foamy head that testified to the liquor's fine quality, Flora's father gave one to each of the players and took one for himself. Before rising and tossing back the drink, the musicians stared fixedly at the bottled citron, because it was well-known that whoever looked at it would keep his eyesight into old age. They strummed on the *thar* strings with a fine feather, producing delicate sounds accompanying the voice of Mahatab Hanoum, the village singer, who was Homa's mother-in-law. By the end of the evening the musicians were completely befuddled, their eyes rolling, Mahatab Hanoum's voice was hoarse, and Flora's father's mustache curled more than ever from smiling so much.

Flora danced with Shahin in the middle of the festive circle and everyone clapped their hands to her and the bells of her anklet tinkled. With her fingers holding Shahin's, she drew him to her and pushed him away, coming close and drawing apart, while the drop of chocolate on her throat trembled and her eyes glowed with laughter and happiness. Shahin held the foot of a wine-filled goblet in his mouth, and rubbed two chunks of sugar between his hands, as if striking sparks from two basalt rocks. The sugar lumps clashed together rhythmically, scattering tiny crystals on Flora's head, whitening her hair and sweetening her life.

As for the dress worn by Miriam Hanoum, the envious guests said that it had come from Herat in Afghanistan, and was chosen after profound consideration. They said that the Baboli bridegroom had been closeted with the filthy she-cat for a whole day, unrolling all the bolts of silk in his stock, until the finicky woman made her choice. They also said that the bridegroom himself took her measurements and cut the material. Her husband, son, and son-in-law wore silk caftans and new patent leather shoes, presents from the bridegroom, who had no family and whose guests were a donkey and an itinerant apprentice.

Flora threw smiles at everyone, as one scatters seeds for birds with circular movements. The spinsters of the village, who had not yet been spoken for, clustered together on one side, drawing consolation from their shared misfortune, and their narrowed eyes pecked at Flora's teeth and eyes. To protect herself and her family from the spinsters' envy of their happiness, Miriam Hanoum shouted during the meal, "Knife! Needle! Pin! Knife! Needle! Pin!"—to pierce the eyes of whoever envied her happiness and sought to harm it.

Even Moussa, who prided himself on his discernment, concluded that evening that Shahin was an honest and faithful man, who would be a good husband to his sister. With his shoulders raised above his neck, and his arms extended in puzzlement in the silk caftan sleeves, he looked like a man who could not think of the answer to a question that had been put to him.

Shahin's donkey was also decorated with silk ribbons and flowers, and the apprentice served the guests with the *ashereshteh,* the dish of noodles, lentils, and saffron that is eaten on special occasions. Nazie had made it for the wedding feast with the proportions of seasoning known to be favored by Reza Shah: very little salt and a good deal of dillweed. But although she had cooked it painstakingly together with Sabiyah Mansour, the *ashereshteh* was somewhat watery, lacking its famous density. The guests turned up their noses and whispered in nearby ears, saying that Nazie had spoiled the dish by stirring it too much, perhaps because of the belief that whoever stirred the *ashereshteh* would soon be wed.

One day, during the wedding preparations, the apprentice had seen Nazie whispering her wishes over the steaming pot, and was emboldened to ask Miriam Hanoum and her husband for the girl's hand. He told them that her cooking had won his heart, but in reality he could not bear to part from his master Shahin.

"We'll have a double feast, two beautiful brides and two honored bridegrooms," he said, his pinhead pupils glittering. Miriam Hanoum snorted in his face scornfully, while her husband explained to him that Nazie had been promised to Moussa from her infancy. Moussa himself grabbed him by the collar, pushed him against the wall, slapped him, and threatened to kill him in various horrible ways, and only let him alone when Nazie pleaded with him to stop.

Before the serving of green kidney beans, which indicate the end of the celebration, and also increase the bodily humors—including those of the male and female who are to join in conception—the guests were given peeled apples and sweetmeats of nuts and cinnamon, to sober the inebriated. While they were eating the fruit, the storyteller of Omerijan told tales he had made up about the newlyweds, and legends about the inhabitants of Babol, who were notorious cowards.

"On the birthday of our glorious king," he began in a sweet, tipsy, breathy voice, compressing his lips in the manner of storytellers, "a contest of bravery and heroism was held at the palace. Every district of our beloved country sent to Tehran a champion who was massive of body and bold of face, and they all gathered in the square before the palace balcony. At a signal from our beloved king, the royal cannons roared and all the war trumpets blared. The terrified onlookers and contestants all fled for their lives. Only two men remained in the middle of the square: the man from Babol and the man from Yazd. But when the king's servants approached them to give them medals for bravery and heroism, they burst out laughing, because they discovered that the Baboli champion had pissed in his pants and the Yazdi had shit his pants from fright, and only their shame had overcome their fear and kept them from running away. . ."

The guests laughed, and Shahin lowered his eyes to the tips of his shoes. His arm had almost healed, and he was dressed in a light-blue caftan with a yellow cummerbund, topped by a green felt bonnet over an elongated skullcap. Scents of soap and perfumes rose from his skin, but they were overpowered by the smell of kerosene from his hair, which struck the people who approached to congratulate him on his bride.

In the first days of his married life Shahin still pulled his member out from between Flora's legs and allowed it to resort to its familiar silk squares. But when his arm had recovered completely, and he took Flora on a ten-day honeymoon in Babol Sar, the cloth merchant became accustomed to his new status and impregnated his wife.

One rare night when the moon was eclipsed, Miriam Hanoum remembered that she had failed to warn her daughter against becoming pregnant on such a night. A girl who becomes a *kuchik madar* on such an ill-omened night was doomed. Flora, like all girls of her age, had heard about the ban, but her heedlessness, her readiness to yield to every temptation, worried the mother greatly. That very night Miriam Hanoum appealed to the demons, who amiably indicated to her that they had received her signal and would grant her entreaty. Nevertheless, the following day she was filled with unease, which turned her stomach. She took pains to vomit three times that day, after the meals, to expel the gut feeling and prevent it from becoming a reality, God forbid. However, to be on the safe side, she also cursed Satan and all his evil angels with deafness and blindness, to ensure that they would neither hear nor see anything when disaster fell. Her husband laughed at her, saying that she was a credulous fool like the damned Zoroastrians, who believed in the sun god and the moon god. But when the young couple returned from their honeymoon, and Flora laughed and snorted at every little nonsense as she had always done, Miriam Hanoum calmed down and forgot her fears and her husband's scorn.

On the morning of Shahin Bozidozi's departure from Omerijan the sky was clear, without a single cloud to worry him. He loaded the owl bag with the few bolts of cloth he had left after dressing the entire Ratoryan family for his wedding, and Flora came out into the alley to accompany him to the southern gate. There she plucked the last ribbons from the donkey's ears and fed it nuts and raisins, to give it strength to bring its master back soon. Shahin promised to come back in two, or at the most three months, and kissed Flora on the point of her black hairline. She pressed him to her heart and held his head between her big hands, and he took hold of the hem of her dress and felt the cloth with expert fingers.

In his eyes, Flora was as beautiful as the blue flax flowers from whose stems his fabrics were spun. The scent of her skin filled his nostrils. She scratched her head, and one of the head-lice eggs he had left in her hair hatched. Her mother and father, Moussa and Nazie, watched her from their window, and Homa and her husband watched from theirs, and the sisters Fathaneh and Sultana from their respective windows pierced the couple with their evil eyes, and the peddlers in the alley and all the other neighbors likewise ogled the newlyweds. Shahin, whose striped robe fluttered in the wind, signaled to the apprentice to stop chewing the nuts that Flora had given the donkey and called out farewell to all and sundry, gesturing broadly with his hands.

A moment before he whipped his donkey toward the Jews' gate, Flora remembered something and uttered a hiccup of alarm. Hurriedly she pulled out a bundle of little silk handkerchiefs, which her husband had asked her to cut for him, folded neatly and scented with rose water. Quick as a thief, with a frown on his large brow, Shahin snatched them from her hands and thrust them into the owl bag. He hugged her and said, his walleye squinting over her shoulder at the snowy mountain peaks, "You're a good woman, Flora. Whenever I use them, I shall think of you, *azizam*."

* * *

But Shahin did not return to Omerijan. He did not come back to see Flora's legs thickening, the veins in her thighs swelling, and the purple blood vessels writhing like snakes and bursting like bubbles on her calves. Her eyelids also swelled and grew heavy from crying. She gouged mourning scratches in her cheeks, and her hair fell out in clumps, until it lost its famous thickness. Even the golden chamomile pollen, which Homa kept for her in a jar with a screwed-on lid, no longer helped, and its chill touch made her skin crawl.

Every morning Flora broke the pissed-on egg under the almond tree in the copse and watched its shell fall apart and the slimy yolk quiver in the light of the rising sun. The village flies were attracted by the tree's mixed stench, and the birds avoided it. Regretfully, Flora gave up eating its sweet almonds, because their taste used to wake up the unborn baby, and its joyous kicks reminded her that her husband had vanished, and there was no man to press his loving ear to her belly.

The days piled up like the mattresses in the parlor in the morning, and an empty space opened up in Flora's heart. She stopped powdering her face in the hope that her husband would suddenly appear on his donkey at one of the village gates, and began to speak of him in a lowered voice, as one speaks of the dead, imitating the speech of the old Ratoryan aunts. Like them, she sighed a lot, shook her head resignedly, and took deep breaths, showing off her premature aging. The smoke of the espand buds, which she inhaled deeply, made her yawn and dawdle more than ever, and she rose from her bed only at mealtimes, to weep and sing her song.

CHAPTER SEVEN

The upturned copper frying pan grew very hot, and columns of thin bluish smoke rose from the burning grease. Using a broomstick, Nazie rolled out the dough on the floured floor. Swaying from haunch to haunch, she rolled it out until it became as transparently thin as human skin, and threw it skillfully over the torrid copper dome. The doughy membrane turned brown and bubbled.

Just when Nazie turned the bread over, dreadful screams were heard from outside, the shrieks of a woman who is not ashamed of her pain and does not try to hide it. Flora raised her head and swung it around sharply, her eyes staring wide open at her cousin. But Nazie, whose ears were attuned to the hissing grease, stood calmly, wiping her hands on the ends of her chador, which absorbed the flour and oil between her fingers. Her head was sunk between her shoulders, the slow, dreamy look was in her eyes, and her mouth hung slightly open.

"*Vavaila!* Nazie, can't you hear? You don't hear what I'm hearing? Listen, listen, somebody's crying terribly." Flora moved her knees away from her belly, which touched the floor, released the entwined swans from the weight of her backside, and grunting with the effort, rose on her legs. But Nazie heard the tortured woman's shrieks only after she removed the incandescent pan from the embers and the noise of the grease subsided.

"Oh yes, I can hear, and how, it must be that Armenian Haidah, the one whose husband sells salt. He must be beating her to death again, poor thing," said Nazie. She was holding the frying pan by the handle, visualizing the man who pushed a cart laden with a heap of coarse salt, its crystals twinkling in the sunlight, shouting with a distorted face: "*Namak! Namak!* Salt! Salt!" Whenever he came into the alley, Miriam Hanoum would quickly throw on her chador, gather up leftover moldy bread, and exchange it for a little salt, which Haidah's husband weighed on his scales. He sold the stale bread for animal fodder.

"Let's go and see who's crying. Come on, dopey, leave that alone, will you…" Flora wound the colorful chador around her head, pressed her hand into the base of her hollow back, and started to walk, pulling at Nazie, who looked around and then bunched up the hem of her skirt before joining her. Reaching the pile of shoes beside the entrance, they fished out their own two pairs, leaning on each other as they shook the insects out of them. Moussa's dog barked at them when they climbed up to the roof. Up there they found that the screams were coming from the house of Zuleikha, the deaf midwife who lived with her husband and old mother on the edge of the quarter, in a little room adjoining the synagogue. The two women had lived there alone until one night a bright-eyed carpenter knocked on their window and asked if he could sleep on their doorstep till morning. The mother, who wanted a match for her deaf daughter, invited him to join the sleeping Zuleikha in her bed, and the man never left again.

"It's some poor woman having a baby. Flora, let's go home, I'm scared," said Nazie. On sultry summer nights the two of them would go up on the roof with the rest of the family, to sleep under the moon with the straw mats tucked under their arms. Nazie and Flora would push their mats close together and fall asleep entwined like man and wife, their dreams shimmering with stars. But now winter had come, a prickly sandstorm danced on the village roofs, and Nazie was afraid.

Flora, who had spent many days on the roof singing to Shahin, ignored her cousin's warnings. Pushing her belly forward, she skipped across the gap, no wider than a child's stride, between Miriam Hanoum's roof and that of Fathaneh Delkasht. From the peacocks' pen rose a clamor of screeches and tail thumpings with hundreds of green eyes.

"Wait for me, Flora, careful with your baby, it'll fall and break, wait for me." Nazie ran after her along the row of Jewish houses, whose roofs were lower, by law, than those of the Muslims, as were their doors—lest they grow proud. The wind twirled little columns of sand, dimming the afternoon light and shaking the laundry lines strung like fences around the houses, billowing out the wash and driving away the birds. Flora stumbled and almost fell into one of the courtyards, but Nazie hurried after her and supported her.

"See, you almost fell. Come on, Flora, let's go back."

"You want to go back, go. I want to see who's crying like that."

When they reached the last roof of the Jubareh, they saw the whore giving birth in Zuleikha's window.

Nazie, leaning on Flora, was so excited she let out a little trickle of pee. Down below she saw the women wrapped in their black chadors, their brows creased with worry, beating their breasts and slapping their fists, indicating to each other how bad things were and how grave the condition of Mamou the whore, who was in such agony. Quite early in her pregnancy, when her belly was starting to peak, they foresaw a difficult labor. But as her belly rose and swelled conelike between her immense breasts, the women in the *hammam* began to say that it was not one of the whorehouse customers who had impregnated Mamou, but the king of the demons of Omerijan in person.

Nazie and Flora held hands and stared aghast at the whore's legs, which were spread open like a fan, with the hole gaping between them like a scream. Mamou was hiding her head in the chador, which stuck to her damp hair and to the scarf tied around her breasts. Her shrieks intensified, the sheets reddened like the sun sinking in the moon gate, and all the neighborhood children gathered around to watch, shouting first from the thrill of discovery, and then from terror. The waves of dust that whirled in the sky above the village like a vast bridal veil reddened their eyes and clogged the spittle that ran from their open mouths. The agitated birds flying over the roofs could not settle down and chopped at the sky with their wings, while from the mosque in the market square rose the sorrowful piercing voice of the muezzin, wailing and making the heart quail. When a head emerged from the whore's body, the children fell silent, and only the wail of the muezzin and the cries of the mother, horror-struck at the baby's appearance, could be heard in the village.

Mamou's fetus had one head with four eyes, fixed in the

hollows of the skull where the ears were supposed to be. When Zuleikha pulled him out, wet with his mother's blood, he almost slipped from her astounded hands onto the flagstoned floor. His four eyes looked at her from his flattened face, and she let out a deaf woman's horrified shriek. One heart beat in the breast, which was dotted with four nipples, and four arms sprouted from his sides. His twenty fingers strained apart. Two tiny members stuck out amid four tiny testicles, and below them twitched four legs. It trembled like all babies, its breath rasping, trapped between the crisscross ribs. Then the single mouth cried out, revealing teeth.

The demon twins shook between the hands of the terrified Zuleikha. The village women held their breath at the sight of the distorted creature crying like a human being. They shaded their eyes from the frightfulness and drove away the pregnant women, to stop them from seeing the dreadful sight, and to prevent the curse of the whore's twins from—God forbid—infecting their unborn babies. Young mothers fled from the scene with their eyes shut tight, moaning in horror and shock, the dust graying their hair prematurely, their children squealing in their arms. Bent old women spun round and round in alarm. Flora looked at Nazie's terror-stricken face and pressed her head to her cousin's flat chest, with its small nipples like knitting-needle studs. Nazie hugged the big body as hard as she could, feeling that at any moment her shell might crack open from fear. Flora twisted around between her clasping arms, tempted to look at the monstrous crossbreed, whose little heart could not withstand the crowd's loathing, and whose single mouth was stilled forever.

CHAPTER EIGHT

T HAT EVENING FLORA ATE
four *gondi* dumplings, which are easy to bite into but hard
to digest. These balls of chickpeas and chicken—which
Nazie had labored all afternoon to prepare, cooking them
in *dombeh* sauce and serving them on a bed of white
rice—are known as a man's dish, good for plumping up
shrunken testicles and rousing limp members. The women
were expected to crumble the dumplings between their
fingers before putting them in their mouths.

Moussa and his father loosened their belts but nevertheless had to struggle to finish the second dumpling.
Manijoun and Homa's skinny husband were satisfied with
rice, basil, and parsley. Nazie poured over the wafer-thin
labash a golden infusion of saffron, and Homa and Miriam
Hanoum crumbled and pecked at a dumpling each. But
Flora, her gaze absorbed and concentrated, ate four of the
gondi one after the other. She wound the chador twice
around her head, tucked its ends under her arms, and
pressed them to her sides to keep it from slipping. Using
her grease-shiny palm curved into a little bowl, she
scooped up ball after ball, pinching their cheeks with her

pudgy fingers, squeezing their crushed flesh, and stuffing them into her mouth. When she finished the four dumplings, she smacked her lips greedily and broke off a piece of bread, staining its whiteness with the yellowish oil on her fingers. She dipped it in the hot sauce until it was soaked, used it to gather the rice heaped on her plate, and swallowed that, too.

She also found room in her stomach for two baked quinces, because her mother promised her that they would cheer up her sad heart. A man who shows a smiling countenance in the morning, Miriam Hanoum explained to Flora, is said to have had a piece of quince put in his mouth by his wife at bedtime. For it is known that the vapor of the quince rises to the sleeper's head, driving away nightmares and sweetening the dreams. Then the men picked their teeth for leftovers and talked about the whore's twins. They were to be placed in a pickle jar with formalin and the jar stoppered, for the disgrace to be preserved for all time and displayed in the center of the village.

Flora broke two pieces off the sugar loaf, placed them on her tongue, and dissolved them in a glassful of hot black tea. As the tea slid down her throat, she seemed to Nazie to be full and contented, resting her back on the soft feather cushions, sighing and breathing heavily. Her legs lay outflung on the Kashani rug, her hands were clasped on her curving belly, and her face sank into her fat chins like a brooding hen. And then, all of a sudden, she demanded watermelon.

Later, Miriam Hanoum, speaking her dead father's language, said that at that moment the house turned from a regulated beehive into a wasps' nest in a hollow tree. Her face turned white, and she exchanged alarmed looks with her husband, daughter, son-in-law, son, mother-in-law, and Nazie. Manijoun was absorbed in her delusions, the contentment of her belly smoothing the creases in her gray face, but the faces of all the others turned as yellow as the remains of the rice on their plates. Their dropped jaws revealed the fragments of sugar on their tongues, and these dissolved quickly in the foaming saliva that they swallowed nervously.

Apart from Flora, who had more greed than sense, whose body was big but her brain small, everyone was aware that it was already early winter and a whole autumn had passed since the red flesh of the last watermelon glowed in the summer heat. But they also knew that a pregnant woman's belly must not be denied, that Flora had to have her watermelon, because if, God forbid, she failed to bite into the fruit she craved, her poor son might be born with an ugly birthmark shaped like a slice of watermelon dotted with black seeds in the middle of his forehead.

Nazie was the first to recover, and she tried to persuade Flora to eat sugared red raspberries, or a juicy pomegranate that she broke open, filling her little hand with its red seeds, or even a plump red tomato that she put before her. But Flora rejected Nazie's fruits and declared that she wanted watermelon, nothing but watermelon. Her black eyes skittered around the room, offended and wavering on the verge of tears, until she succumbed to them, broke down, and cried bitterly. She bit the back of her hand, sucked the skin between her lips, and rocked back and forth like a man praying.

Homa caught Flora's earlobe with its silver hoops between her fingers. Large and crooked, she stood over her, pinched and pulled the earlobe as hard as she could, and threatened her with such a beating on her beautiful body that she would have a better reason for crying. Moussa marched up and down the room, stopping in every corner to cough throatily, and roared about honor and shame. Flora's father knelt before his daughter and tried to distract her from the taste of watermelon by telling her horror stories about the cholera and smallpox epidemics that hit the village when she was a little child. Homa's husband scolded him in his droning voice, saying that such stories could harm the baby's appetite when it grew. Miriam Hanoum went from room to room, wringing her hands and calling down curses on her dead father, wishing that a herd of oxen would trample on his grave and efface his memory. She knew that on that night, a Wednesday night, the demons held their weekly feast, and on that particular Wednesday they had a special occasion for celebration because their king had just fathered a monster son on Mamou the whore. To divert them, she sent Nazie to fetch a bucket full of cold water and emptied it on the front doorstep, to placate the demons and restore calm to the house.

Manijoun, too, became agitated. The shouting around her reminded her of past events, and she sat up in her basket, her face full of cracks like the wall, and rolled her eyes to the ceiling. She repeated the story of her dead daughter, the little sister of the twin butchers, the fathers of Flora and Nazie. They were triplets at birth, and when everyone was shouting for joy at the birth of male twins, out came the female who had been waiting patiently in the back of the womb, and gladdened her mother's heart.

"*Khodaia!* God! That's all we needed now—your

daughter! *Zakhnabut,* suffocate and keep quiet, lunatic!"
Miriam Hanoum told her off tensely. But Manijoun did
not listen to her and, like a woman revealing her secret
pain for the first time, talked about how long her daughter's hair was and how thick. When she was seven, the gentile barber tied a handkerchief around her neck, carefully
shortened the black tresses, and then nicked the delicate
neck with his scissors, and the child died of her wound. As
if in remorse for telling her story, the old woman clutched
her head, covered her ears to avoid hearing her granddaughter's watermelon wails, and her tears dropped into
the basket between her crossed legs. She tugged her silvery
plaits, seeing the barber's laughing face and his hand outstretched for the money.

"Watermelon, I do so want a watermelon, Mother,
Mother...," Flora howled mindlessly.

"It's the middle of winter and the middle of the night
and she wants watermelon!" yelled Moussa, his face distorted with rage. "I hope she gets a little watermelon
face with seeds all over it, like the pockmarks on ugly
Nosrat's mug!"

"*Baha, Baha, mashallah,* that's what comes of all those
pumpkin and quince jams you feed her, all the rose water
Mother makes her drink for the sweet smell," Homa
shouted, her eyes popping. "Now she thinks she is the
queen of Persia." Homa's husband said again that this is
what happens when you marry a daughter to someone
who is not one of us. "He passed by your window and
peeped in, and right away you made him a member of the
family. That's what happens when you pick your bridegroom off the street, that's what happens."

"*Vavaila,* stop! Stop talking so much, and Flora, dear

heart, *azizam,* you should always have flowers and pistachio nuts falling on your head and down on your feet, stop
crying, shhh…," Miriam Hanoum pleaded, but she did not
go near her daughter to hug and comfort her.

Moussa yanked at his sobbing sister's hair as if to uproot
it, pulled up her head, and butted it. "Look, just look how
stupid you are. If you don't stop crying this minute, I'm
going to smear a piece of dog shit like that husband of
yours on your forehead, and bring the mirror from
Mother's room for you to see how dumb you are, you
piece of shit…" Moussa's voice choked, and the pimples in
his face almost burst. When he managed to draw air into
his lungs, he spat in her face, and the saliva trickled down
with her tears.

"I want watermelon…," sobbed Flora, who heard nothing, not even her own cries, which seemed distant and dim
like someone else's cries. Nor did she wipe the spittle off
her face, only bit her lips and sucked them between her
crowded teeth, which left a crooked mark on the flesh of
her mouth.

"Pay the money, you dirty Jewess, your pretty girl is
waiting for you outside!" Manijoun shrieked and sank into
her basket, keening softly, brooding on eggs that would
never hatch.

"Enough, enough of your screams, God carry you off,
all the Jews have gathered outside…," Miriam Hanoum
shouted at her mother-in-law and pinched her nipples as
if trying to twist them off. She went up to Flora, took the
kerchief from her head, and wiped the girl's running nose.
"Enough, come now, enough crying, blow hard, hard!" she
said, pumping Flora's nose. Then she wiped her face and
tried to soothe her with soft words. But Flora went on

sniveling, and Miriam Hanoum began cursing again, wishing that all her daughter's mornings would be as black and evil as this screeching night.

"What could I do, *azizam,* when he slaughtered my little girl?" Manijoun asked the air above her. Her arms fluttered and flapped like a bird's wings, while her hands tried to tear the girl's plaits from her head.

"Look, precious eyes, just look what a hole you're making in your mother's heart, maybe you'd like…" Miriam Hanoum's husband ignored his mother and spoke to his daughter in a soft voice that could hardly be heard in the commotion. Gently he stroked Flora's disheveled hair with his butcher's hands, and his face grew red from the effort of self-control. His trousers, which were pulled up over his belly, revealed their short, roughly sewn hems, uncovering his girlishly thin ankles above the slack socks. His mustache with its silver threads bent its sad smile toward Flora. Occasionally he shaved his mustache, which grew as thick as his greasy hair. Without it her father's face looked naked to Flora, and with it like a stranger's.

"What she wants is for that husband of hers to push between her legs and give her what she needs. What she needs right now is for us to shove a hot skewer into her, maybe then she'll calm down a bit and behave herself…," Homa suggested, demonstrating with her hands. "Right, Flora? *Khodaia,* God, I hope your baby comes out squinch-eyed like his swindler father, amen and hope to God, you should have a baby like Mamou's, exactly! We'll see if he'll bring you watermelons in the middle of the night, you bonehead! Rub, rub your backside on the floor until it burns and smokes, then maybe you'll calm down a bit, you dumb bonehead!"

"Homa, shut up!" screamed Miriam Hanoum. "How you talk and talk! I hope your tongue tree goes up in flames and burns to the ground, damn that cursed tree that opened your big mouth. Shut up a minute, the Jews are like cats in the alleys. Shut your mouth!"

Homa did not speak until she was five, and was believed to be mute. Her mother gave her mustard seeds to chew every morning, but they did no good. Finally one spring Miriam Hanoum traveled all the way to Isfahan, to pick a leaf from the forty leaves that sprouted every year on the tree of tongues. These leaves, which were meticulously counted, were red and perfect, elongated and rounded at their tips, remarkably like the human tongue. A healer from Isfahan had told her that if a mute drank wellwater that had been boiled with a leaf from the tree of tongues, his throat would open and his tongue would start to move. But, he repeated, not more than one leaf.

But Miriam Hanoum picked three leaves, boiled them in water, and gave it to her daughter to drink. A few days later Homa's little mouth opened, and she shouted her first words. "Corn on the cob! Corn on the cob!" she yelled, imitating the cries of the hawkers in the alleys who fished yellow cobs from the steaming tubs. From that day on, Miriam Hanoum would say angrily, the girl never closed her mouth. She talked and talked, and there was no end to her chatter.

Moussa could no longer stand the female commotion around him, Homa's jealous sermons, Flora's howls, Manijoun's insane mutterings, and his mother's pleas and curses. Full of bitterness, he went out into the cold Jubareh with a vase-sized silver goblet in his hand, to fill it with the neighbors' saliva for Flora to drink. It was a particularly efficacious dervish charm against the evil eye, and his mother decided the time had come to use it.

In the dark, Moussa's hound looked like a wolf. He followed his master's tense body, pouncing on every odorous cat and chirping cricket on the way. He did not understand that the game Moussa was after was the evil eye, which had got into Flora. It started to rain, and the two of them dripped water as they stood in the doorways of their neighbors, who woke up blinking from their sleep. Moussa bent under the low lintels and asked every neighbor to spit into the goblet. Fathaneh was wide awake, waiting for him with her forced smile, and spat with pleasure. Nor did the other neighbors resent the intrusion, but stretched their mouths in a great round yawn that ended with an eager smile. "What do you need a cup of spit for now, Moussa?" they asked, their eyes glittering, avid for juicy tidbits of gossip that they would serve up to their own neighbors. They all swore that it was not their eyes that had driven his sister mad, then they hawked loudly and dropped their turbid foam into the cup.

After Moussa left, Homa limped over to her skinny husband, gathered him into her bosom, and the two departed in nervous silence to their house. On her way to the door, she hit her sister lightly on her head twice, then bent down, and pinched her thighs.

"Go on to your house now, Homa. Out you go now," Miriam Hanoum said to her, waving her hand.

"Good thing she's gone," she sighed in some relief when her daughter left.

Nazie knew that it was not greediness or self-indulgence that made Flora crave watermelon, and she busied herself removing the stains left on the rug by the raspber-

85

ries, pomegranate, and tomato. Once Flora's brother and then her sister had left the house, she hugged her cousin and stroked her belly with the thorough, circular movements she had used to clean the fruit stains from the rug. Flora's cries gradually subsided, and Nazie felt that her palms were slowly overcoming them, their rounded rhythm setting the pace for the sobs. The big body snuggled gratefully up to the small one, and Nazie almost suffocated under its weight, but she did not budge and controlled her movements. Whenever a circle was less than perfect Flora perceived that she had been slack in her howling and promptly stepped it up. Nazie stared glassily at the embroidered pattern on the Kashani rug, which she had never worked out, as it always seemed to grow more intricate before her eyes whenever she tried to follow the endlessly writhing forms. Flora wearied of crying and waiting, and her howls of craving for a watermelon subsided into low murmurs of despair.

Though Nazie pitied Flora, she was more concerned for the welfare of the baby, on whose forehead a stain was just then forming, and whose father was absent. She tucked her head into the hollow between Flora's breasts and softly begged pardon of the demons that were raising the baby in her cousin's belly: *"Farhiz...farhiz...farhiz..."*—in the manner of mothers who ask permission of the demons that look after the sleeping baby to move it from its cot to the bed, so they would not be annoyed by the intrusion and would not put bad dreams into its head.

Eventually a watermelon with white stripes on its green shell was found in a cellar. Flora's shrieks had woken ugly Nosrat from her sleep, and her kindly heart remembered the days when the girl's laughter and snorts and her warm smell had filled the kitchen. Dressed only in her night-gown, she went down to her cold cellar and took out from behind the wine barrels a watermelon that she had stored there to keep it from rotting. When Moussa reached her house and knocked on the door to ask her and her husband to spit into the goblet, the watermelon was waiting like a pregnant belly between her hands.

It was a wild watermelon that had grown on the edge of the cultivated fields of the Dashti Kavir, the great salt desert in the middle of the country from which no one who ventured in ever emerged again. The watermelons, which grew on the edge of the desert, were watered nei-ther by rain nor by rivers, only by the morning dew, which fell on the vines and quenched their thirst, sweetened the fruits' flesh, and increased their price. Wet with rain and red in the face from groveling, Moussa also held the water-melon like a pregnant woman holding her belly and urged ugly Nosrat to come to the poultry shop the next day. He promised to give her two ducks, their combined weight equal to that of her watermelon.

When he stood on the threshold, even before he closed the door behind him, Moussa struck the watermelon with his hand and the striped shell burst. His fingers tore open the crack, exposing the red flesh. His face was contorted with revulsion as he threw a chunk at his sister, much as he tossed to his dog at the end of the day leftover pieces of fat and bones from the birds he had sold.

Nazie moved away from Flora, who lusted for the fruit as for her husband's kisses, biting into it furiously and chewing its flesh. Her blood seethed as it had not seethed that night in the Babol hotel room with the sunflower wallpaper. Her backside slid from the cushions onto the rug, and the whole family watched as she gathered the chunks of watermelon into the hollow of her crossed legs and put them to her mouth, biting again and again while the red juice ran from the corners of her mouth. But the chill of the cellar in which the watermelon had been stored did not cool her blood.

Miriam Hanoum was the first to speak. "Please God this watermelon will cleanse Flora's blood of all the poisons Shahin had put into it, and the demons will stop tormenting her," she said, and her husband added, "Please God, please God." But Flora did not hear, she only bit and sucked and let the red juice drip on her wrists and elbows and on her dress. When she finished, there were only white shells left between her legs.

In massaging Flora's belly to calm her, Nazie had been infected by her cousin's craving for watermelon. When Moussa broke it open, her eyes grew round with envy, her nostrils flared, and its aroma touched her throat. When at last only shells were left, Flora burped aloud, and they all thought that she was feeling better, but a moment later she had a bellyache. She ran outside to vomit on the stinking almond tree, and Miriam Hanoum said that her stomach hurt because of the whore's cursed baby and because of the evil eye—only this time she did not have Fathaneh and Sultana in mind, but Nazie. They had all seen her eyes widen and her tongue licking her lips. Nazie veiled her eyes, gathered the striped shells that were scattered on the rug, and withdrew shamefaced to the kitchen.

Before throwing the shells into the rubbish sack, she scraped with her fingernails the traces of rosy flesh that remained on them. She licked and sucked her fingers and looked back in the dark, to make sure no one saw her. But there was no one there, they were all bent over Flora who was leaning on the almond tree with her hand. They cursed Shahin and his donkey with insomnia, talked about the treachery of the Babolis, and commiserated with poor Flora.

Nazie, too, wanted to go outside and say poor Flora and what a shame, but her eyes filled with tears and she did not move. All she could think was—poor Nazie, shame about poor Nazie. Flora had in her belly a pink baby and a red watermelon, its black seeds being vomited at this moment under the tree. In Nazie's belly threads wove themselves together into a thick winter garment. She pressed the shells to her mouth because she wanted to yell that she, too, craved watermelon, that she, too, wanted fruit of a different season, that she, too, wanted Moussa to go out with his hound and bring her from the neighbors a bowl full of peaches, plums, and grapes. The watermelon shells slipped from her hands. She stood and listened to the harsh retching in the garden, followed by the splashing vomit and the family patting Flora's back and tut-tutting.

Through the curtain of colored wooden beads that hung in the kitchen doorway, Nazie could see the face of the queen of Persia. She was gazing wearily at the girl from her regular place in the entrance hall, which was also the parlor, the dining room, and Moussa's bedroom. The queen's portrait was woven of cheap woolen threads, black, green, and white. The craftsman who had woven the delicate moon face had no red wool with which to make her thin cherry lips. He had coiled her raven's wing black hair on top of her head, wove her famous green eyes very closely, but left out her mouth. In Nazie's eyes, the beautiful barren queen looked sadder and older than ever.

Nazie tore her own gaze away from the unsmiling queen's face, washed her flushed face in the water bucket, so that her envy would not be observed, and went to bed to check if her wish had been granted. Shivering from the chill of the bedding but full of hope, she curled under the wool blanket and searched with a finger between her legs. The finger came out clean, no blood on it. Still, she licked it, but there was no hint of a strange taste, only the usual taste of her body and with it the trace of watermelon. Again her eyes overflowed, and with the tears came the image of the rabbi *mullah* Netanel, the matchmaker, shaking his old finger at her and muttering that she must hurry, because time is a-wasting. The image of the women who washed their clothes when she did in the *hammam* looking at her askance, as if the blood was already flowing between her legs but she was not telling. Their thin plucked eyebrows rose higher and higher in their foreheads, and their mocking voices echoed in her ears.

CHAPTER NINE

On WASHDAY MORNINGS
Nazie would pack the dirty clothes into bedsheets and
knot their corners together just as she knotted the ends of
her kerchief on the top of her head. Moussa would come
home from the shop, hump the bundles on his back, and
Nazie followed him like a beggar, picking up the socks
that dropped out. When they reached the lane that led
from the market to the *hammam* and farther toward the
mountains, Moussa would stop, raise the load high in the air,
and drop it with a thump on the flagstones. Nazie insisted
on going the rest of the way to the *hammam* by herself—
so that the women would not gossip more than they
already did, she said.

There she divided the heavy bundles into smaller ones,
flung them over her bowed back, and carried them one by
one, until they made a big heap at the feet of the woman
gatekeeper of the *hammam*. She would wipe the sweat from
her brow with her forearm and shade her eyes from the
sun's glare to see Moussa watching her from his hiding
place in the sheepfold, bent double, waiting for her little
smile. He crouched among the bleating lambs and watched

as she paid the woman gatekeeper, took off her felt slippers, tucked them under her arm, and disappeared into the underground bathhouse.

Wednesdays, as well as the early hours of every morning, were the regular bathing times of the demons and spirits who lived in the village. The *hammam* was left empty for them. Anyone who wandered accidentally underground during the demons' bathtime reported that he heard them blowing bubbles in the water like children, and a chant of "blub-blub-blub" rose from the baths. But on other days of the week the place thronged with human beings. At the end of the week the men would entrust their heads to the barber at the *hammam*, who groomed their locks or polished their pates, and they would plunge into the hot pools and moan with pleasure: "Ahhh, that's good…oh, so good…*Baha, Baha*, wonderful…" Sundays, Mondays, and Tuesdays were the women's days.

During the morning, long slender shafts of light filtered in through the wall slits like God's fingertips. The sun's rays revealed the dust motes dancing in the air, broke in the water pools, and cast pale reflections on the stone walls. In the corners where the water was hot, the women bathed their bodies. From there the water, now tepid and dirty, drained into the laundry pool.

The bathhouse attendants kept the steam going by throwing bucketfuls of water onto stacks of heated stones on the hearths. Nazie loved the vaporous fog that covered her face with sweat. Like the other women, she padded her knees with straw against the hard stone floor. From the soap seller, whose cries of "Soap! Soap!" echoed hollowly, she bought two greasy lumps, pushing her finger into them to check if they were good and dry. If the soap was damp, she would haggle with the peddler and knock the price down.

Looking for a spot to kneel on, Nazie tried to keep close to the Tamizi women, the laundresses who washed the clothes and bed linen for the wealthy village wives. They were silent and industrious, because this was their living. There were four Tamizi women, with smooth, shining faces and ruined hands. The bent old grandmother would give the wash its first dunking in the pool. Her daughter would scrub the clothes with soap, one granddaughter rinsed them again, and another wrung out the clean wash and stacked it in a heap. But one day Nazie had seen Shahnaz Tamizi, the rinser, turning her head at Moussa in the poultry shop, as if admiring herself in a big mirror, and since that day she avoided her and her family and worked alone.

Shahnaz hid her pockmarked cheeks in the chador while carrying the *kachakul* basket her mother had given her to fill with slaughtered chickens. Inside the dusky shop her face gleamed like a pita spread with egg yolk, and her black hair looked soft and shiny. Standing under the tenterhooks, Moussa caressed the black hair with his eyes, but Nazie wanted to seize and pull it sharply until Shahnaz grimaced and screamed.

The women liked this day of washing and bathing. Though they worked hard until evening, dunking and scrubbing and wringing clothes and linen, nevertheless, it was a day of contentment and ease, of chatter, singing, and laughter. They would put the babies in the shallow tubs and at the end of the day take them out wrinkled like old people or newborns. Far from masculine eyes, they would strip quite naked, their breasts swinging from side to side, letting the steam soothe and purify their skin. They smeared black and red henna on their hair, with pomegranate rind and egg yolk, and tied it up with a piece of muslin, until it turned the color of tea leaves and gleamed. They rubbed each other with olive oil mixed with ground almonds and other nuts to sweeten their skin. The *hammam* maid walked among them, and for a penny she would scrub their backs with a loofah and beat them with bundles of sage. She rubbed their feet with black basalt stones, peeling the hooflike skin. Now and then she passed among them with a tray, offering glasses of chilled *faloudeh,* a sweetened whipped starch drink with chipped ice.

The women chatted endlessly, discussing the husband whose lust was insatiable, the daughter who had the runs and the heaves, the boy who refused to be weaned and was driving his father mad with his screams. As they talked, they cracked salted watermelon and pumpkin seeds, so that by the end of the day their sandals were buried under a layer of moist shells. The best-kept secrets in the village were discovered in the foggy steam, the pregnancies that had been painstakingly hidden under dresses were revealed, and every rumor was verified. The unmarried girls strutted like the Delkasht peacocks, showing off their taut bodies, the nursing mothers pampered their sucklings with milk warmed by the steam, and the barren women bathed their bellies in the bowl of keys, a consecrated recess carved out of the *hammam* wall. Forty copper keys, greening in the water, covered the bottom of the niche, one for each of the most fertile women who had ever lived in the village. The barren woman's mother would pour forty tumblers of water into the niche and bathe her daughter's sealed belly, whining piously for her womb to open so she would bear many children.

Nazie took no part in the women's commotion, she did not even join their shrieks when they discovered a boy who had climbed up on the roof to feast his hungry eyes on their nudity through the glazed portholes. She did not unbutton her dress all morning, and gray flowers of sweat bloomed under her arms. She undressed at the end, when the washing was already drying on the stones above the bathhouse. Bashfully she took off her dress and washed herself quickly under the thin stream.

The more she withdrew into her work and silence, the more the women teased her with their inquisitive questions. They called her by the mocking name Nazichi, little Nazie.

"Where is Moussa, why isn't he here today to help you carry the wash?"

"Don't you have a tummyache, Nazichi? Go and check, Nazichi, go check…"

Fathaneh and Sultana, who saw through their respective windows how Nazie slaved for her aunt, whom they both detested, pitied the orphaned girl and said her period was delayed because Mahasti, her blessed mother whose soul was in paradise, was descended from the Levites, and it was known that the period of Levite women was a sacred one that arrived late, sometimes only when they were wed. The kindlier women agreed with them, but others said that she would never menstruate, that Nazichi would never be a *kuchik madar,* a little mother, because she had been born prematurely, and it was plain to see that she had a child's body.

Ever since Homa buried her baby and pregnant Flora was abandoned by her husband, the women did not bother to lift the curls from each other's ears to whisper behind a discreet hand about the Ratoryan women. Their loud voices, which echoed from the sweating walls of the *hammam,* made Nazie's little body cringe, overwhelmed her heart with their malice, and haunted her all the way back to her aunt's house. Only when she worked alone in the kitchen did the droning voices subside, but they never fell quite silent.

The women counted Nazie's misfortunes on their fingers, clucking and looking at her reproachfully: she has no parents, her aunt has appropriated her dowry, not a drop of blood has dripped from her hole, and she is as thin and flat as a sickly chick. These things were true, and they caused Nazie sharp and prolonged pain. But when the women made up tales to amuse themselves, amazed by the horrors of their own invention, Nazie's pain quickly vanished. They said that forbidden acts were going on in the house of Miriam Hanoum, who was too lazy and perhaps too wicked to put a stop to them. The slanderers bit their clenched fists with horror, begging God's pardon for allowing their innocent ears to hear what their mouths were saying—the things Moussa Ratoryan did every night to his little orphaned cousin, under the protection of his mother, that darling of the demons, who nightly brought her onion skins that turned into gold bracelets, and because of whose childhood sins the cats never stopped revenging themselves on the village.

"*Aoundareh,* poor little orphan," they would sigh, glancing at Nazie sorrowfully. "At her age one should be counting chicks, and she has not even laid the first egg, poor thing."

"Without Flora's big tits, God carry her off she's so

pretty, the children Moussa gives Nazie will surely starve…"

After soaking for hours in the murky water, Nazie's hands were as pallid as the faded old bedsheets, and their skin was dry and peeling. She looked at her reflection in the pool and drowned the women's falsehoods by stirring the washing in the water and causing whirlpools. The sound of the ripples overcame the noisy chatter, and Nazie bit her tongue.

Part Two

NAZIE WANTS
TO SLEEP

CHAPTER TEN

WHEN NAZIE WAS BORN, HER body was so tiny that the local healers clapped their hands in amazement and refused to treat her, saying that the demons wanted her as a toy for their children.

That was what Sultana Zafarollah told Nazie. Having seen through the gap under the roof that Miriam Hanoum had left the house and Flora had disappeared into one of the neighbors' kitchens, Sultana would climb up to the murmurous dovecot on her roof, select a plump, rosy-frilled pigeon, and bring it to Nazie who was working in the kitchen. Lingering in the kitchen to wring the bird's neck and pluck its feathers, she would tell Nazie stories about her dead mother, Mahasti, all of which Miriam Hanoum would later dismiss as a lot of nonsense.

The year Nazie was born, germs of smallpox spread in the currents of the village canals in which the children splashed, barefoot and laughing, all summer long. It was said that the Shiites returning from their pilgrimages to the holy city of Mashhad had brought the contagion to the foothills of the Alborz and the cities of the coastal plain. The Shiites used to take their lunatics to Mashhad, where they tied them to a mosque or a saint's tomb to restore them to sanity. The addlebrained returned with clear heads, and their relatives with strengthened faith, but they brought the disease in their blood. When the seeds of death spread to Omerijan and the surrounding villages, they struck the Muslim inhabitants first and then spread like a breeze to the other neighborhoods.

The disease flowed with the sewage in the street, flew with the mosquitoes' stings, and swarmed in the rats' teeth. It easily overcame the fortifications of the Armenian quarter and bloomed repulsively on the skin of the Jews who lived amid the almond trees. In the early days the Muslims thought that the disease was sparing the Jews, because of the wine and beer they swilled all the time, but their envious fury subsided when cries of pain rose from the alleys of the Jubareh, and there, too, wails of bereavement slunk like homeless cats.

The villagers hung red cloth in their windows. They wrapped the afflicted in deerskins and blankets that had been steeped in tubs full of wine and beet liquor. The women stuck red feathers in their hair, sprinkled chicken blood on the rags in which they bundled their babies, and smeared earth, date paste, and henna on their cheeks. The wealthy ones decorated their houses with red gems, and everyone wore scarlet ribbons around their wrists and necks. At sundown the whole village turned rosy and crimson with the blazing color that stirred the blood to protect people from the plague. Draped in a fiery-red robe, with a woman's red woolen headscarf tied around his white *amameh*'s bonnet, his face smeared with rust-colored henna but his lips pale with fright, *mullah* Abbas, speaking from his pulpit, informed his florid congregation that the disease was maddening its victims' blood because one of the dead who was buried in the village land was chewing his shroud. The villagers dug up the graves on the hillside to find the guilty corpse and make him stop nibbling on his shroud and dragging them after him into the ground. A bad smell of corruption hung in the air, and the English hospital, a day's walk from Omerijan, filled with twitching patients whose faces bubbled like the millpond under a heavy rain.

During the plague year childbirths were difficult and noisy. The women's wombs shrank and produced stillborn, yellow, and bloated babies. Babies who insisted on being born alive emerged from their mothers' bellies tiny and feeble, lacking the strength to cry, and most did not survive their first day. Premature Nazie survived in her woven palm-frond cradle, but remained tiny. On the advice of Miriam Hanoum, Mahasti rubbed her black nipples, enlarged by frequent childbirth, with clear royal honey, but the milk and honey that Nazie sucked did not spread sweet infantile fat under her skin. At the age of six months she weighed no more than a seven-month fetus, and her big almond eyes bulged in her pallid face like the eyes of tadpoles. Rabbi *mullah* Netanel the widower told Mahasti to feed her verses from the Book of Psalms, which he wrote on slips of paper, and to keep whispering threats in her ears, to urge her to grow. The neighbors advised her to feed the baby crumbs of sheep's entrails stuffed with rice and swimming in fat, which made all the villagers lick their fingers in anticipation. But nothing helped. The healers who had refused to treat her were astonished by her pointless, prolonged existence and waited for her to die.

"*Vavaila!* Not yet dead, that little one? A garlic skin is

thicker than hers, how come God hasn't taken her yet?" said the women in the gardens of the Jubareh. Many of them had lost children in the epidemic, and their sharp eyes glared at the palm-frond cradle that Mahasti had woven for her daughter and pierced the minute infant who clung to life. "She's no bigger than a newborn bat," they said, delighting in Mahasti's terrors. "It must be some cursed creature of the demons, God send it to all our enemies...Poor little thing, she doesn't have enough strength to draw breath from her nose into her body...Come wintertime she won't have enough flesh on her to protect her from the cold. No matter how close you hug her to your breast, Mahasti *azizam,* the mountain winds will carry her off, don't you see? Go give your husband some sons, and let this poor little thing die."

"Catastrophic storms are approaching," the women prophesied with their eyes shut, "blowing on Omerijan from the frost on the mountains and shaking the earth. They say that whole forests are being uprooted like little shoots. They say that roofs fly off like hats, and clothes, God help us, are torn off people's bodies like wash off the laundry line and disappear in the wind...This year everything will be carried off by the storm, and what the storm doesn't take, the earth will swallow into its belly, like a hungry husband coming home..."

"*Ya Khodaia,* O God..." Fear of the quaking earth made the goggle-eyed women tremble, and they bit the soft flesh between thumb and forefinger. The old ones clasped their knees and wailed that they could feel the approach of the hellish cold in their old bones.

Surrounded by the Zoroastrian amulets that Mahasti had hung on her cradle and the blue chicken eyes that

Miriam Hanoum had set in silver and hung round her neck, covered by four red goats' hair blankets, Nazie gazed at her mother with enormous eyes, amused by her amulets, jewels, and dresses. Mahasti had conceived four times since her marriage, and had borne four daughters, all dead. Constantly tucking the four blankets around Nazie's neck, she bent over them until they turned salty from her tears. In her heart of hearts she, too, believed that the demons would not let Nazie live but would give her to their children.

But the winter was an ordinary winter, and the earth also contained itself and did not open its maw. But one morning when Mahasti untied the cocoon of blankets and diapers in which Nazie's tiny body was bundled, she saw on the transparent skin of her daughter's throat the pus-filled boils of the deadly disease blossoming like evil flowers. The world turned dark. She lowered her head into the cradle and tore at her hair.

"That one died on you, too?" said her husband when he heard her weep, and got up to beat her. But Mahasti was already beating herself, pinching the thin skin on the backs of her hands, slapping her own cheeks, and hitting her breasts.

"*Khodaia,* what shall I do now, *Khodaia?*"

"So that one died on you too? You stubborn woman," her husband raged and hit her on the head. "When will you give me my sons, when? Look what a weak belly you have, you filthy woman—daughters, lousy daughters, that's all you can bear. Please God you'll die soon, too, stubborn like your mother and ugly like a demon. Another woman, I know, I need another woman, a woman with hot blood who will give me sons. A woman, are you? Disaster is all

105

you give me with your cold blood. You chill my seed like rain, you do, all those dead girls coming out of your womb, you bitch...," he roared and kicked at her legs, and Nazie, alarmed, shrank between her mother's breasts.

Hearing the screams, the neighboring women left their houses and their noisily waking children, veiled themselves, and went to Mahasti's house. They guessed what had happened and called one another out of their dark kitchens, while their tongues practiced words of consolation. "Pity on you, child, *na kon,* don't do this to yourself..." They formed a sorrowing ring around the woman who bent over her crying daughter, scratching her cheeks till they bled. Their hands caressed the air above her head.

"Go away, whores," Mahasti screamed at them, raising the naked Nazie and shaking her, displaying her sores. "See what you've done with your evil eyes, God blind you! Go away, go to your children and your husbands, go!"

"Leave them alone," hissed the father. "Shut your mouth, bitch." He took his daughter from his wife's lap and coolly examined the swellings on her skin.

"You pity me, do you?" Mahasti jumped up and snatched Nazie from his hands. "You don't have any pity for my daughter? Didn't you say she would die when it snowed? But I sealed the windows tight, you snakes, and kept my daughter warm with blankets, and fed her warm milk from my breasts—why should she die? Why? It wasn't the cold that got her, it was your evil eyes that sneaked through the blankets like ants in the wall. It was your bad words, whores, which cursed me and my daughters, curse you! Go, go, your lives should pay for hers, the poor little thing..." She broke down crying and the tears drowned her words. The offended women wrapped themselves in their chadors and flew from her yard like alarmed birds.

"Shame!" Nazie's father roared when they left. "Shame is all you bring me, you whore! It's the devil in you. I've seen you at night opening your legs, you whore, for all the demons of Omerijan to come and impregnate you with the devil's seed. Devil daughters is what you give me, dead, all dead, like you should be tonight, you bitch!" But Mahasti had pulled herself together and stopped beating herself, because Nazie was crying harder. She knelt down at her husband's feet and pleaded with him to put his coat over his head and go and call the Armenian doctor and rabbi *mullah* Netanel the widower to come and save her daughter.

The man relented and left. But, as his wife had feared, he walked slowly, hanging his head in resignation. The passersby who greeted him did not see an anxious father rushing to find a doctor to cure his sick daughter. His bowed back suggested a man unhurriedly searching for a gravedigger. His heart, full of bitter thoughts, gradually closed and stilled, and he dawdled in his search.

Alone at home, Mahasti wept quietly about her stubborn husband, about the wickedness of the women in their windows, and about the dark sky. When Nazie's whimpering grew weaker, her patience snapped. She crossed the alley, fell on Miriam Hanoum's neck, showered flattery on her, and begged her to follow her husband's crawling pace through the snow.

"And if you don't find him, *azizam,* take pity on me and go to the shop, ask your husband to look for the son of Janjan *Sabzi* Furush, and bring the doctor here quickly. Go, Miriam Hanoum, go and God will bless your legs, please go now."

"Let the girl die." Miriam Hanoum pushed her off. "Such a short and miserable life she's had, your daughter, and if she lives, Mahasti, who will have her? Only a cripple or an idiot would take your daughter, hadn't she better die now?"

"She'll live, you'll see, she'll live…," wept Mahasti, and the tears scalded the scratches on her cheeks.

Miriam Hanoum poked her red-hooded head into the alley and looked up at the sky. A strong wind whirled the snow, and black clouds rested on the dentated village walls facing God's angry countenance.

"If she lives," she said, withdrawing back inside and looking at Mahasti with clouded eyes, "if she lives, I'll give her my Moussa for a husband. I make you this vow, Mahasti. But Nazie won't live because she wants to die, I can already see a little smile of relief on her poor lips which don't even want to suck at the breast. It's only thanks to you, Mahasti, and your tireless hands, bless them, massaging her chest to open the way for her breathing— because her lungs are still closed like an unborn baby…Can't you see she's underdone, like a partly pickled eggplant. I ask you—"

"Go, I beg you, go fetch the son of Janjan, she's going to die, go…," Mahasti pleaded.

Finally Miriam Hanoum went out into the alley. She left Flora at home with Moussa and carried the seven-year-old Homa in her arms into the cold. Her shoes sank in snow and mud, but she did not catch up with the father because, like him, she did not believe that the baby girl would live to see another day, which was why she did not hesitate to promise Moussa for Nazie.

They found the Armenian doctor at the house of the

Jewish miller, Pinhas. The miller had been dying for days, lying with his mouth open and his tongue swollen. Loud wails rose from his house, and the garden filled with neighbors sighing and mumbling the dead man's praises. Nazie's father and his twin brother and Miriam Hanoum with Homa in her arms pushed through the mourners and entered the darkened house.

Pinhas's wife and daughters, their dresses ripped, keened over him, while his daughters-in-law set copper pots filled with water on the stoves. His sons and sons-in-law sat in stunned silence around the covered corpse, listening to rabbi *mullah* Netanel speaking uneasily about the burial arrangements.

The Ratoryans tracked mud and ice into the house. Speaking softly, they said some words of consolation to the bereaved family and then asked the son of Janjan *Sabzi* Furush to come and look at a dying baby girl.

"All right, all right, wait outside, I'm coming..." He waved them away, frowning. Whenever he was called to look at a patient, he grumbled about the family's exaggerations, which described every cough as consumption and every itch as leprosy. He ran his fingers through his hair which, like his mother's hair, smelled of herbs, put on his furry coat and packed his leather bag. Janjan had saved every penny she could spare from the sale of mint and basil to send her son to the medical school in the capital. After serving for many years as a doctor in Reza Shah's army, he returned to the village, highly conceited, and became its most eligible bachelor. He was obliged to take two wives, one a Jewess with common sense and the other a Muslim with body sense, and spent alternate nights in their beds.

The doctor rubbed his hands in camphorated oil and

sprinkled Nazie with sharp-smelling vinegar. Then he bent over her, felt her swollen neck, and immediately declared that there was no hope, the baby was about to die. Mahasti, who was looking up at him in terror, burst out crying again. Miriam Hanoum pressed Homa's head to her breasts to protect her from the approaching death. The doctor wrapped Nazie in her diapers and, submitting to the inevitable, put on his sheepskin coat. Like the rest of the village dwellers, he did not believe that such a tiny, frail creature could resist the dreadful disease, and was surprised that she had survived so long. Nazie cried till she almost choked, but he did not change his mind, and when Mahasti moved to pick up and cuddle her daughter, he pushed her aside impatiently, as if she were a tiresome fly buzzing about the room.

Everyone stared at the grim-faced doctor as he exchanged a few quiet words with Nazie's father. Silence fell in the room, and they all stood still and tried to listen over Nazie's and her mother's crying and the chuckling of the demons' children rubbing their hands in anticipation. Suddenly they heard the clamor of Pinhas the miller's funeral approaching the almond tree alley. The neighing of the horses pulling the death wagon mixed with the keening of the women. Mahasti was astounded to see the doctor grab Nazie with one hand and rush out into the alley.

"Na-azie!" she cried and sprang to her feet to run after him, but her husband caught her in his arms.

"Don't move, I swear on my life I'll kill you with my bare hands, I'll strangle you, stand still!" He pressed one hand on her mouth and with the other grasped her squirming neck.

Outside, the doctor stood upright, raised his free hand

in the air, and stopped the funeral procession. The lamen-
tation of the women overcame the mournful howling of
the wind. The alleys of the Jubareh were narrow, and the
mourners, who huddled close together against the chill
wind, trailed in a long thin file like ants. They were carrying little oil lamps with flickering flames. They still had a
long way to go, but their curiosity overcame their grief,
and they stopped to listen to the doctor. The widow and
the mourning women around the death wagon stopped
scratching their faces and pinching their breasts. When the
cries fell silent, rabbi *mullah* Netanel motioned to the doctor to speak up, because they were in a hurry. The doctor
waited a moment longer until they were all looking at him
in silence, hats in hands, as if he carried God's words in his
leather bag, along with the iodine and smelling salts, and
was about to read them aloud.

"My dear fellow villagers," he started, making a grand
gesture with one hand while continuing to shake the crying Nazie with the other. The people narrowed their eyes
and stretched their necks the better to hear him over the
whistling wind.

"Merciful people, this poor infant is the only daughter
of Ratoryan the poulterer, and in a few minutes she is
going to expire. She is trying to get her soul out of her
body and return it to the Creator. And since the angel of
death has already come down, *ptui*"—the doctor spat
sharply through the gap between his front teeth, to cool
down the overeager demons, and the mourners spat after
him—"since he has already descended from heaven to the
village, and taken the soul of the poor miller, and his six
dark angels are waiting up there to carry out God's will…I
therefore ask permission of the honored rabbi not to hurry

to the cemetery while the angel of death—*ptui, ptui, ptui*—is laboring to take this infant girl's soul out of her body. Let us wait, let him do what he needs to do and then set out again. This is what I beg of you, sirs."

He turned solemnly, his hair white with snow, to the relatives of the dead man, who were standing abjectly behind the rabbi. "This deadly plague is exhausting us, sirs. We run to the cemetery the way a man suffering from diarrhea runs to the privy. Wait an hour until the poor thing dies, and let us bury both unfortunates, may the God of us all have pity on them both. Why should we exhaust our strength making this journey four times in twenty-four hours? The strain would kill us instead of the disease. And let us spare the six dark angels, who may take pity on you…"

The mourners grinned wryly. The doctor's plea entered their hearts. The black crowd pushed and shoved closer to the Ratoryan house, like a swarm of ants around an over-turned beetle. They stopped the death wagon opposite the house gate, and the doctor laid Nazie in a hollow he dug in the snow with his hands. The snow melted around the feverish little body. Pinhas's relatives settled limply on the low stone wall. The accompanying mourners placed the oil lamps near them, spread their caracul coats on the frozen surface, sat down, and listened to Nazie's obstinate crying, waiting for it to cease.

A pair of vultures circled overhead. The smell of the dis-eased corpse rose above the crowd, some of whom began to chatter and smile as the reason for their gathering in the almond tree alley faded from their minds. Others paced up and down through the standing and seated crowd, their heads bowed, their expressions grave, hands clasped behind their backs. The brilliant green market-flies buzzed among them. The children gradually slipped away from their mothers, pulled the knitted red caps off each other's heads, threw snowballs, and fought, until they were separated and once again shackled by their mothers' clutching hands. When one of them happened to sneeze, unaware that sneezing during a funeral attracts the dead person's misfortune, his mother pulled five hairs from his head until he shrieked.

Suddenly Mahasti burst from the house. On the way out she grabbed two quacking geese, as white and fat as clouds, and ran shrieking into the alley. Her eyes stared and her lips trembled. She ripped open the throats of the struggling birds and her fingers tore the fat flesh apart, white feathers flying in all directions. Blood squirted out, spattering her face and hair. Dirty eggs fell from the bellies of the geese and broke whitish on the reddening snow.

"Here, Jews, take! Take!" she shrieked and flung the warm flesh to the crowd. "Take it for a sacrifice and go do your burying in the cemetery!" Dogs fell growling on the dripping pieces of flesh and tore them with their fangs.

"You want another death, you lazy Jews? Here then, God carry you off, here—take it and bury it! Why do you suddenly want my poor daughter? What happened? She's all skin and bone and boils. All of two kilos, and burning with fever. Take these fat geese instead, they're ten kilos each, and leave my daughter with me, to die in peace..." The mother's voice broke, her tears mingled with the blood on her face, and she collapsed on the snow beside the fighting dogs.

"*Aoundareh,* poor woman," Mahasti heard the villagers murmuring pityingly. "God preserve us, she's gone mad from all those daughters, the poor woman…" But no one moved to leave, they all sat on and watched.

With her face buried in the snow and her husband standing over her baring his teeth, she suddenly noticed that the baby stopped crying.

Mahasti jumped up in alarm, ran to her daughter, and shook her to make her cry again. But Nazie's eyes were shut and she did not utter a sound. Mahasti pressed her ear to the tiny bruised chest and heard the heart beating strongly, as if trying to jump out of the rib cage into her ear and share its secret with her. Mahasti also closed her eyes, put the tiny dying baby on her shoulder, and slunk like a mourner after the barking dogs deep into the alleys.

Nazie owed her life, said Sultana Zafarollah, her eyes filming dreamily, to mute Sherafat, whose solitary wisdom and melancholy advice saved her from the disease, so that she lived and grew to a height of a meter and forty centimeters.

Mute Sherafat was an adept of mysteries and could read the future in the clouds, but she made little use of her knowledge. Only rarely did she talk to the villagers, being absorbed in her own wrinkled soul most of the time. She had not been much of a talker even in her single days, but she adopted her fishlike silence only after she married fragrant Yacoub, the perfumes and cosmetics seller, who also traded in healing stones and crystals. Every evening he returned to his house in the almond tree alley with his mustache and chest hair redolent of women's scent like an adulterer. When they got into bed, Yacoub would try to entice his wife, but the perfumes awakened her jealousy and suspicions and she would turn her back to him until he gave up and fell asleep. Only then would Sherafat turn to him, pressing her ear to his to listen to the rustling of his dreams, and grind her teeth till morning.

In her vexation Sherafat ground her teeth so hard, as though crushing her rage between them, that they broke and crumbled and she spat them out like traces of food. Her gums were left bare and her empty mouth shriveled like an old woman's. Sultana said that Sherafat lost her sense along with her teeth and, to prevent anyone seeing what she had done to herself out of jealousy, she shut her empty mouth and fell mute. Eating only soft baby foods, she grew thin and ugly, and her fragrant husband began to betray her with the Muslim girls who came to anoint themselves with his scented unguents and to add precious stones to their silver rings.

On the night when Nazie's mother appeared in her doorway, spattered with the blood of the geese and holding her dying baby in her hands, mute Sherafat opened her mouth for the first time in many years. An ill, rotten odor rose from her throat and the syllables fell out heavy and unclear, but the words were plain enough.

"Go away." And she slammed her door in Mahasti's face.

"Open up! Open up! By your life!" Mahasti banged on the door with her fists.

The mother's cries were loud and persistent, and Sherafat went out to silence her with a piercing look. Her husband was fast asleep, and her mind was searching through the names of the women he made love to in his shop. To avoid waking him, she pulled Mahasti and her daughter into the house. A strange mixture of perfumes and incense hung in the air, and the dusty shelves were laden with jars filled with poppy bulbs, opium infusions, and human embryos preserved in a cloudy fluid.

With dull eyes and tight lips Sherafat took Nazie from her mother, wordlessly spread a sheet on the carpet and undressed the baby. Mahasti crouched over the naked Nazie and gently rubbed the infected skin. Sherafat took crinkled peach stones from a jar, cracked them in her fists and roasted them in the burning oven. Then she took the seeds that nestled inside the hard shells and pounded them in a little spice mortar. The room filled with a strong scent of peach blossom. She mixed the crushed seeds with jasmine oil from one of her husband's bottles, and with her open palms applied the thick paste to the baby's thin body, rubbing it thoroughly, letting the skin absorb the fragrant oil, concentrating gently on the open boils. When their discharge was wiped with a piece of cotton wool, Nazie pouted and began to cry again. Her feverish flesh heated the glistening oil on her skin and caused the peach paste to ferment. Mahasti's hot tears fell on the jasmine oil while Sherafat decorated the baby's face with great care, as though working on a painting. She smeared her lips with bright red paint, shaded her eyes and outlined them with kohl, and reddened her cheeks with turmeric.

"Like a virgin bride," mute Sherafat whispered to the mother, who was gazing at her daughter in a trance. Though Sherafat's voice was as brittle as a twig, it woke her sleeping husband from his dreams of market girls, and he came into the room dressed in a checkered nightshirt, burning with old love for his wife, whose mouth had suddenly reopened. Sherafat motioned him back to bed like a sleepwalker and dressed Nazie in a tiny white gown. Then she tensed, her face grew solemn, and very carefully she ripped the collar of the little gown along its seam. Mahasti's heart suddenly misgave her, because she knew that Sherafat was closer to the demons than anyone else in the village, and for a moment she feared that by tearing the collar she was opening their way to Nazie's soul.

"Now," said Sherafat, the words hissing like embers in her mouth, "leave her with me and go to your husband to make sons for him."

"What will you do with her, Sherafat, eh? What will you do with her?" stammered the young mother, as if her mouth, too, were unused to speaking, and turned to look at her daughter who was made up like a tiny whore.

If the demons' children want her for a plaything, explained mute Sherafat, growing breathless from so much speech, scorpions will sting her and hedgehogs will prick her, and she will die. But if they don't want her, Nazie will be found in the morning with her ripped gown neatly sewn and spotted with blood from the demons' fingertips. Then she will recover and grow and will be a healthy happy *kuchik madar* like all the girls.

Hearing that the baby would spend the night lying on her back in a lime pit full of yellow scorpions and pointy-faced hedgehogs, Mahasti jumped out of her skin. She snatched her daughter from the carpet, tore the white gown off her, and rubbed the baby's painted face to wipe off the vivid colors and their evil spirits. The mother's saliva mixed with the lip rouge, eye shadow, turmeric, and kohl, and ran into the sores in Nazie's skin.

Sherafat tried to speak, but Mahasti refused to strike an alliance with the village demons. Once again she flung the baby over her shoulder and went out, not knowing where to go. Crickets chirped in her ears and the houses were shuttered and dark. In desperation she ran through the alleys howling: "My daughter! My daughter! God, kill me and give life to my daughter!" Her eyes being shuttered by loneliness and tears, she stumbled and fell.

Mute Sherafat, her tongue dry and white, her hands oily and redolent of jasmine and peach blossom, came out after the wretched mother, took the baby from her hands, and brought them both back to her house. After binding Mahasti's bleeding feet with clean strips of burlap, she proposed a different method of healing her daughter, so that Nazie would recover, grow up, marry, and have children.

When the sun rose, Nazie's exhausted mother dragged her bruised feet back to mute Sherafat's adobe house. In one hand she held Nazie and in the other a big fish-basket filled to the brim with worn leather sandals and torn felt slippers. At the wise woman's behest she had gone from house to house, her eyes lowered, and like a beggar collected shoe after shoe—men's, women's, and children's shoes, mostly odd ones and hardly any pairs. Their combined weight in the basket roughly equaled that of Nazie's bones. Sherafat laid the coughing Nazie on the scales and lightly tapped the boils on her skin with branches of rue, for their potent scent to drive away the demons and spirits that squatted with her on the pan to confuse the scales. When the naked baby was quite hidden by the leaves, Sherafat took the shoes one by one from the fish basket and threw them on the opposite pan. When the scales balanced, she covered her empty mouth and said to Mahasti: "Now take your daughter and go to sleep. This child's life has been saved, and nobody wants to take her away from you."

CHAPTER ELEVEN

WHEN NAZIE WAS FIVE YEARS old and weighed fifteen kilos—about as much as the meat that Omerijan housewives bought for a big festive dinner—her parents died of food poisoning, and her father's twin brother persuaded Miriam Hanoum to take in the orphan girl. She addressed her aunt as *ameh bozorg,* great-aunt, but she called her uncle Daddy, because his face was one with her father's. She missed her mother dreadfully. Whenever Miriam Hanoum's husband saw Nazie's triangular face looking sad, he would take hold of her sharp chin and shake it lovingly until she smiled, then he pinched it, as though trying to pull off the tip of the inverted triangle. Finally abandoning the chin, he would kiss his fingertips loudly.

When Nazie was six, Flora said to her: "Go away, this is not your house, this is not your mama, this is not your daddy, go away!" Moussa in his rough boy's voice told his sister to shut up.

In the year of the great drought, when Nazie was seven and did not yet know that she was intended for Moussa's bed, he sneaked one morning into the emptying coop of the Muslim chicken breeder and stole a solitary egg, which glowed at him like a whitish oval sun. That year all the cisterns failed, the lakes dried up, and the fishponds vanished. On the bottom of the channels surrounding the village, under the broiling sun, twinkled silver coins that had fallen over the years from the hands of children. Even the brackish pools in the valleys turned into dazzling white salt pans, driving the thirsty and hungry people to despair.

At that time quite a few rogues were found out who converted in turn to Christianity, Islam, and Judaism so as to receive food, clothing, and money and, having run out of religions, ended up wandering hungrily through the alleys. Many of the region's villagers migrated that year to Shahrud and Babol, hoping to find some employment in the silk industry, but this, too, failed when the silkworms died, and the mills were reduced to weaving cotton and linen.

In that year of famine the demons of Omerijan did not pamper the village housewives with double and triple yolks in the hens' eggs. Most of the hens perished of hunger and thirst, their combs having turned blue from desperate clucking for water. The few eggs that reached the village stalls were imported from overseas, like huge pearls nestling in cotton waste. The merchants sold them to the fishermen, who sold them to itinerant peddlers, and by the time they reached the poultry stalls in Omerijan, they were mostly rotten or cracked, and cost as much as a young chicken in a year of plenty. Only the wealthy were able to celebrate the annual *No Ruz,* the traditional Zoroastrian rite marking the day when the bull that bears the world on its head transfers its weight from horn to horn. A mirror was placed in the middle of the cloth spread on the carpet, and on it as many eggs as there were people present. At the moment when the new year was born and the bull threw the world from one horn to the other, cries of joy broke from the rich households that had been privileged to see the eggs tremble momentarily on the mirror together with the whole world.

In his flight home Moussa ran through the bazaar, bumping into people who crept about despairingly. The merchants did not sing the praises of their goods but wearily shook twig brooms to chase away the flies and begged their hungry customers to fill the folds of their robes and chadors with merchandise. The villagers poked mounds of squashy-rotten vegetables, sniffed with disgust at the heaps of open-mouthed fish, and gazed blankly at the stringy beasts and birds suspended from the tenterhooks.

When Moussa reached his parents' house, trembling with excitement like a tyro thief, his breath was short and scratchy and he could not utter a word. Nazie turned to go and make him an infusion of jasmine flowers, but he stopped her and made her put her hands together, curled like a little nest. He looked around to make sure no one saw them and let the egg slip from his sweaty black fingers, which had almost crushed the thin shell, into her cradling palms. Nazie's eyes shone at the sight of the precious egg that was laid in her hands and glowed white in the dim kitchen. Moussa folded his hands around Nazie's, and the two crept without a word behind the house and hid among the rosemary and laurel bushes. The blue rosemary flowers got into their hair, the scent of the laurels filled their noses, and the reflection of the egg in their black eyes was like a white pupil.

"Let me hold it again," Nazie pleaded when they had stood in silence, looking at it for a long time. Moussa rolled it back into Nazie's cradling hands. Again and again they moved it from the black bedding of his hands to the warm hollow of hers, huddled together like brothers with pleasurable secrecy. Then they decided to bury the egg in the sandy soil under the pomegranate tree, to dream that night about hard- and soft-boiled eggs, and eat it the following day. They were not to tell anyone about it, not even Flora.

The next morning, when Miriam Hanoum rolled across the bed to the side of her husband, who had already left for the empty poultry shop, when Homa rolled over on her back, Flora on her side, and Manijoun snored in her corner, Moussa and Nazie took the egg from its burial place, washed off the soil of the pomegranate tree, and danced excitedly around their booty. Nazie boiled a little water on the charcoal stove, as she did every morning, and carefully placed the egg in it. Moussa peered over her shoulder, and his pimply face was reflected in the bottom of the copper pan. When the egg white had set and the yolk was done, the egg danced in the pan, butting against its sides, and the water rolled around it with big, jolly bubbles.

Moussa shelled the egg carefully and cut it in half. When he saw the yolk, yellow as the midday sun, his breath rattled with excitement. He swallowed saliva and ordered seriously: "Bring me the salt, Nazie." Nazie obeyed him, and when she placed the glittering salt bowl before him an idea glittered in her mind.

"Put a lot of salt on it, so there'll be a lot, enough for both of us," she said, her toes twitching in her felt shoes and the saliva filling her mouth. Moussa followed her advice, took a pinch of salt between his fingers and sprinkled it, took another pinch and sprinkled it, and then another, to increase the bulk of the coveted egg. The layer of salt on the egg was so thick that the yolk halves turned white as full moons, but the children's eyes shone like four suns.

Moussa swallowed his half whole, spat it out with distaste, and then vomited everything he had eaten the night before. Nazie stroked his back from the neckbones to the tail, poured him a glass of tea from the samovar, adding mint leaves and lumps of sugar candy, which is said to help digestion, and stirred the drink until it cleared. When Moussa had drunk it and recovered, the two of them took the remaining half of the egg and reburied it under the pomegranate tree. Since the year of the drought, and to this day, Moussa does not like to season his midday omelette with salt, content to use a little pepper and cumin, and when he sees Nazie sprinkling glittering salt crystals on the moist beans, his heart fills with love and laughter.

From inside her woolen blanket Nazie could hear Miriam Hanoum preparing tea with mint leaves and sugar candy for Flora. The stirring spoon rang in the glass like a clapper in a bell. Miriam Hanoum added to the drink the saliva of the envious neighbors, which had been collected in the goblet, and stirred again to submerge its white foam in the black tea. Before sending Flora to bed, she gave her a sprig of rosemary to put under her pillow, calling it "a besom of paradise," like the old women who believed that rosemary sweeps the sorrow from the body, until it is cleansed like the souls of those who dwell in paradise. Nazie thought that Flora did not need a sprig of rosemary under her head but a wash with soap and water, because when she entered the room, she brought with her a bad smell of watermelon vomit, and her hair glistened in the dark as though it had been rained on. She huddled on the mattress beside Nazie and sobbed quietly like a little girl until she fell asleep.

Even as she slept, Flora continued to utter soft whimpers, which came and went like the wind in the windows. Her cheeks were round and bulging, as though she had stuffed them with food for an imminent journey, and her eyes were shut tight, surrounded with puffy bluish rings.

Nazie moved her face away from the wall, because the voices of the family echoed in the stones and seeped through the layers of clay between them. She imagined the dull sound of the words sinking slowly through the foundations into the ground, trickling into the water wells, rising again in the buckets, and filling people's mouths when they drank tea or soup. The voices gave her no peace, like the image of Shahnaz Tamizi smiling at Moussa in the shop. But she was more worried about the demons who were toying wickedly with the baby in Flora's belly. To pacify them, she stroked the round belly, which looked in the dark like an overturned hump, and begged their pardon: *"Farhiz...farhiz...farhiz..."*

Then she snuggled down in the woolen blanket, making herself small, because she was missing her mother so much. Her belly felt as if it contained a prickly clump, like a bird's nest entangled with twigs and threads, leaves, and feathers. She drew her short legs up to her chest, pinched her earrings between finger and thumb, and prayed quietly with dry lips, carefully enunciating every syllable. She had been given the gold earrings—a pair of elongated fishes with a minute coin bearing the likeness of Reza Shah in his tortoiseshell breastplate—by Miriam Hanoum on the day she learned from her how to cook *hormeh sabzi,* a winter lamb dish that was Flora's father's favorite. No sooner did the autumn rain fall, than he began to speak longingly about its tart flavor.

When the lemons, the *sabzi,* and the meat were bubbling on the charcoal stove, and wonderful odors and smoke rose from the chimney, Miriam Hanoum passed a needle through the fire and threaded it with a white linen thread that she knotted.

"Now shut your eyes tight," she said to Nazie. "I'm going to add one other thing to the pot, but you're too young to see it."

Nazie obeyed and covered her eyes with her hands. She smelled the lemon peel stuck under her fingernails, and her nose sniffed curiously to discover the mysterious seasoning. Miriam Hanoum said in a low sweet voice that on the morning of her wedding day she would lift the hair from her ear and reveal to her what she had added to the dish. Then she pushed the needle into Nazie's earlobe, hard, as though stitching a thick fabric.

Nazie bit her tongue with pain when Miriam Hanoum pierced the other earlobe and passed the linen thread through it. Both ears bled profusely, like samovar taps, and the threads turned red. The *hormeh sabzi* was forgotten, boiled and turned sour, and Nazie burned with fever. Her stitched earlobes swelled and looked like unshelled hazelnuts, filled with pus. Only after several days of deafening pain, during which she was treated with ice water and mint leaves, could they untie the thread, which had been tied too tight. They kept the dried pus in a jar, and Miriam Hanoum finally inserted the fish earrings, symbols of fertility, into the healed perforations. But all the village women, knowing that Nazichi had not even had her first period, made fun of the gold fishes dangling from her ears, and the young ones swished their backsides at Moussa's avid eyes and laughed.

Unable to fall asleep, she repeated the bedtime prayer, slowly and more clearly than ever, for God to hear over the windy rustling of the almond trees and the ululations of the demons who were celebrating the birth of their new offspring. Shahnaz Tamizi's white teeth shining in the dark poultry shop gleamed before her eyes under the woolen blanket. She kept pressing her earrings between finger and thumb, to indicate to God exactly what she wanted Him to do—make the blood come out between her legs so that she could marry her cousin Moussa.

CHAPTER TWELVE

Ever since it was rumored in the village that the Muslim nurses at the English hospital were snatching newborn Jewish babies, hiding them like bundles of dirty washing in the laundry baskets, and smuggling them out of the hospital, the women of the Jubareh went back to giving birth at home, as their mothers had done.

When labor pains began and persisted, and the woman had been laid on a rug in her parents' home, a child would be sent to bring fine sand to soak up the blood and another to fetch Zuleikha the deaf midwife. When she arrived, all the neighboring women would come in, too.

With her heels pushing against the birthing stones, her buttocks up in the air, with her mother and sisters sweating as profusely as she did and supporting her so that she would not fall over, the woman was free to curse her husband to her heart's content. Zuleikha knew when to push her knee into the swollen abdomen, a hand's breadth below the navel, to make the baby's head come out. If the woman writhed in labor for many hours to no avail, the midwife would announce in her raw voice that the demons were calling her to come quickly to deliver their babies. She would take off her apron, as though ready to leave, and hide behind the door with the other women. Left on her own, the terrified young woman would shriek harder, advancing the birth, and when the head began to emerge, Zuleikha would return and pull the baby out.

At that moment, when its bald head was out while its body was still gripped by the pelvic muscles, the midwife declared the sex of the newborn without waiting to look between its legs. If the baby emerged face up with its eyes open and searching, she knew it was a male child. And even before the body with its tiny member appeared between the mother's thighs she would pronounce the preparations for the circumcision rite:

"Go to the market," she would carol in her loud, awkward voice, "slaughter a cow, rip out its intestines and sprinkle salt in its blood...la la la, *hoy hoy hoy*—we've got a boy...stuff the intestines with rice and pine nuts, sew them with needle and thread and give...la la la, *hoy hoy hoy*—we've got a boy..."

Hearing the song of male children, the women in the next room would join in the singing and go out into the Jubareh to fill the village with joyous ululation, announcing the boy's birth and singing his father's praises. Sometimes the new mother's bliss on hearing the singing was so great that the hot afterbirth leapt excitedly up to her lungs and suffocated her to death. This was why Zuleikha customarily pricked its fine membrane with a heated needle while it was still inside the woman, without waiting for it to emerge slowly in the natural way. She dabbled her fingers in the thick dark fluid that dripped from the afterbirth and used it to draw circles on the foreheads and cheeks of any barren woman present.

But when the fetus emerged from its mother's belly facing the earth, with the back of its head to the midwife, she knew that another female was coming into the world. Even before she held the wet baby, she would round her mouth, shade it with her hands, and utter a piercing long wail: "Hoo...hoo..." And when the neighboring women, whose ears were pressed to the door, heard the jackal wail rising from the room, they, too, would round their mouths and hands and join in the keening for the poor mother who had borne a daughter.

It was enough for Zuleikha, the deaf midwife, to see Nazie's tiny head emerging from her mother's tunnel to know that it was a female and to utter the female wail. Mahasti had heard the sound four times, and each time it was cut short, because the little girl was born dead.

But Mahasti did not need to hear Zuleikha wailing to know that she had a daughter. Ever since she found she was pregnant, she knew it was not a son she was carrying. Four times before she had had that bad feeling in her belly, and this time she was determined to empty her womb before her abdomen rose like an anthill and the pregnancy became known.

When the embryo was three months old, the mother circled the village of Omerijan seven times, as if chasing the tail of a cunning demon, and when she returned to her house in the almond tree alley, sweaty and exhausted, she drank a jugful of apple vinegar.

Sultana Zafarolla stroked Nazie's gloomy face and told her never to doubt her mother's love for her, because Mahasti's heart had wearied of her husband's threats. He had vowed that if she bore one more daughter, dead or alive, he would kill her and take a new wife, one who was strong and obedient, whose belly was sturdy and blessed, who would bear him sons.

"You are something else, *azizam*," Sultana said to Nazie. "You're not Flora. She's like a soft-boiled egg, but you're a hard-boiled one. You hung on to the walls of your mother's womb and you didn't fall out—not even when your mother rolled herself down the wet stairs in the *hammam*, God preserve us, all the way to the bottom."

For when Mahasti stood up, her underpants were dry and the embryo had not fallen into them. Its obstinacy strengthened her resolve. If he were a boy, he would not have clung to life so, but would long before have slid into the latrine. Time was running short; her belly threatened to push through the covering clothes and reveal itself to Nazie's father. She went to the husband of Fathaneh Delkasht and asked him to pluck the longest feather from the tail of his largest peacock. Fathaneh's ears opened and turned red, because she understood Mahasti's design, and at once told her sister about it. Mahasti dipped the hairy feather in a half-filled bottle of arrack until its royal blue turned black, the green eyes turned blue, and the silver freckles green. When the feather was quite soaked in arrack and a powerful smell of aniseed turned her head, she remembered her distant wedding day and began to cry quietly.

She knelt on the carpet, leaned backward with her knees apart, and loosened the waistband of her dress, which she had previously tied as tight as possible on her navel in order to strangle the baby. She also raised her thin underskirt and exposed her gaping nakedness. The shutters were closed, and a yellow butterfly that found itself imprisoned in the dusky room fluttered like a lost soul between the walls and watched what she did. Mahasti pressed on her rounded belly in order to see the red hole between her legs. With her heels in the air and her knees trembling with terror, she pulled the feather from the arrack bottle, held it by its stem like an inverted writing quill, and pushed it into her body, until she felt the fine hairs tickling the nose and neck of the forming female. With one hand she twisted the feather and with the other she stirred the blood that flowed on her thighs and trickled into a red pool on the carpet. She rubbed her bloodied fingers all over her body, her face, and her hair, until she passed out.

When she was found, all covered with blood, Miriam Hanoum and the neighboring women did not know where it was coming from. Expecting to find the wound on her head, they dipped a cloth in cold water and cleansed her face, searched through her hair looking for cuts, wrung out the cloth and passed it over her back and her belly, which had begun to swell—and then, when they turned her over, they discovered the stem of the peacock feather sticking out between her legs, like a red flag.

Her crime was exposed, and all the villagers talked about her wickedness and pitied her poor husband, whose wife sought to kill his children. Mahasti armored herself in silence, which was variously interpreted. Daily the learned doctor, the son of Armenian Janjan, passed his listening tube over her belly and frowned at what he heard. He ordered her not to leave her bed unless the house was on fire. But every time Mahasti saw smoke rising from the chimney of her neighbor, Goli Psar Zaideh, the mother of sons, she would quietly get up, slip out of the house, and secretly peer through the window of the fortunate mother.

It was not because Goli's cooking was so appealing that Mahasti stood on tiptoe and peered through her window, nor was she driven by the whims of pregnancy, which confound the appetite. Goli Psar Zaideh had borne her six sons in the secrecy of her house, behind the doors that she barred and the windows she shuttered as soon as her labor pains began. Quietly and with self-restraint she bore them, without a midwife, without curses and the chorus of envious women. Before going out into the alley, she would stuff a bundle of rags under her dress so that they would not know she had given birth, and pretend to be still pregnant, resting the small of her back on her palm as though feeling the weight, and sighing. To Mahasti, peering in through the window, Goli's sons with their red hair and cheeks looked like brilliant carrots and pumpkins, and their color fueled the burning envy in the heart of the mother of dead daughters. Goli pretended not to notice Mahasti's prying eyes but quietly whispered things to urge the demons to harm her. Returning to her house, Mahasti would refuse the honey and dates, butter and bananas, which Manijoun told her to eat, and made herself a meal of basil and celery with dry bread together with some potatoes swimming in fat—like the meal she had seen through Goli Psar Zaideh's window.

Nazie was born in the middle of a torrid summer Saturday. The air was redolent with the odor of Sabbath eggs hardening in the *hamine* pots, luring down the people who had gone up on the roof in search of a fresh breeze. The Jewish families gathered in their houses, mildly soothed by their cool walls. The men dozed, full-bellied, mustaches shining with grease, bodies slumping as sleep overcame them. Only Nazie's father did not sleep. Withdrawn in his childless house, he prayed to God to let him have a son at long last. The neighbors' children peeped through windows, and the women went out one by one into the almond tree alley, carrying pots of charcoal. With honeyed tones they asked passing gentiles to light a flame for them. Having found a beggar willing to help, they set the charcoal pots in a row. The gentile put a burning ember in each pot and fanned hard until the coals caught fire. While he was doing this, the women's tongues wagged about Mahasti, who was writhing in labor pains.

When the women's wail rose, carried by a gust of hot heavy wind, Nazie's father went out to the stable behind his house, lay down on the ground with its straw and manure, and hid his head between bags of hay and bran. His horse swished its tail above him, its hoofs stamped on the ground, and white foam bubbled between its teeth. When the neighboring women came to console him and bring him cooked dishes, he drove them away with curses.

The women's wail passed from house to house, emerged from the Jubareh, and reached the village square, to the house of Mamou the whore with its low roof, green doors, and black crows perching on the windowsills. Mamou smeared blue henna on her plucked eyebrows, pressed her breasts together with wires, and went to the almond tree alley. Behind her swinging backside walked two of the girls she had bought at birth from their disappointed fathers and raised in her house. They were seven years old, almost as fat as she was, and their eyebrows were also plucked and painted blue. When the three approached

Mahasti's house, the women at their windows clucked and shook their heads. Coming out of their doorways, they said to each other: "Better for this baby girl to die and join her sisters than to grow up at Mamou's to be a little whore, *vavaila,* God spare us…"

The horse neighed and stamped when Mamou's breasts burst from her neckline into the stable. Her painted face was streaming with sweat. She threw a cloth bag filled with coins at the feet of the father who was lying prone in the corner. When the bag hit the ground, the coins gave a jolly, metallic tinkle.

"If that poor little daughter of yours weighs more than a kilo and a half," Mamou shouted at Nazie's father, "I'll give you another bag like this one. Just don't try to teach old Mamou her business." She laughed in the loud voice of a fat woman and slapped her own buttocks to prove her point. "But if she weighs less, you'd better keep the female to yourself. God knows I don't need little sickly Jew females to stink up my house. I got nothing to do with them later…," she added and nodded at the seven-year-olds who stood behind her, to show him how plump and healthy they were, in case he wanted to comfort himself with one, or perhaps with both of them together.

But Nazie's father got up, and speaking in the broken voice of a father mourning his son, asked the whore to leave him to his grief. When the whore smiled at him shrewdly, convinced that he was pretending so as to raise the price, and again indicated that he could make use of the girls, he uttered a dreadful howl. He fell on Mamou and her protégés with blows and curses, driving them to the end of the alley, where they escaped with dusty dresses, straws in their hair, and broken red fingernails. He returned to his house full of rage, threw out his mother Manijoun and his sister-in-law Miriam Hanoum, and while his wife lay hurting and bleeding from childbirth, he turned his back on her.

CHAPTER THIRTEEN

Homa was fatter than Flora, her breasts were swollen from lust, and her thick arms were powerful. When she was sent as a child to gather kindling for the fire, she ripped whole branches from the trees. One day, when she and Flora were still children, they climbed up on the roof and together they squatted and urinated. The two yellowish streams mingled, shimmering in the sunlight, and flowed together into the rain gutter, ringing like a rusty tambour, and ran into the foul street ditch. Then the two of them rose on their toes and shouted nonsense into the mouth of the chimney, so that Nazie, who was sitting in the kitchen shelling peas, would think that demons were speaking to her from the oven. "Naa-zie...Naa-zie...," the chimney echoed weirdly. The soot blacked their hands and the olive skin of their faces. They untied the string of a kite that Moussa had made for them from brown wrapping paper and thin wood slivers.

As soon as the string was freed from the hook, the kite filled with life and rose ecstatically to heaven. Homa rose on tiptoes and, with her arms outstretched and her hands together, ran along the roof struggling with the wind. The serpent of colored ribbons that Moussa had attached to the kite's tail also teased the sun's rays, writhed between them, and leapt happily up and down like the two sisters. Entranced, the girls shaded their narrowed eyes with their forearms and peered at it from under their elbows.

"Nazie, hey, Nazie you dope, you must come out, come and see, come out, Nazie!" Flora shouted into the chimney, and ripples of laughter echoed her words. Nazie left the peas and went outside, wrapped in an apron, and standing in the shadow of the house she looked for the girls on the roof but saw nothing. With her back to the almond trees and her face to the sky, she walked backward, step after step, until the colorful paper serpent flew out madly before her eyes. Below it she saw Flora, her face blackened, hopping from side to side, and Homa holding the end of the string, looking down at her and falling from the roof to the ground.

The next day Moussa went up on the roof and built a low parapet from wooden beams, which he sawed and planed. Homa, lying indoors, heard his hammer beating out rusty nails, which he straightened and brightened. She sweated inside the heavy plaster cast in which she had been encased from her heels to her waist by the expert bonesetter, and screamed that she was going mad. All day until the sun went down, she felt swarms of stinging ants on her skin while the hammer banged on her head and summer blazed throughout her body. In the evening Moussa came down to eat, and Homa fell asleep.

At the end of the summer, when Zuleikha's husband came to cut off the sweat-and-grease-blackened plaster cast from Homa's legs, he had difficulty sawing it because she had grown very fat. The sharp metal teeth scratched her skin, which had paled from olive to almond in the course of the summer. When the saw finished scraping through the plaster and the white dust had settled on the floor, Homa tried to walk. She moved a tremulous leg toward the outstretched arms of Miriam Hanoum, who murmured, "Come, Homa, come," but the other leg collapsed under her, and she fell on her face like a baby and burst into bitter, offended tears. Miriam Hanoum stood over her daughter and looked at her legs. Her face in its braided frame did not move, her lips were tight, and her eyes hard as nails as she bent over her weeping daughter and stroked her face gently. Seeing that Homa was comforted by her love, Miriam Hanoum took a deep breath and slammed both fists on Homa's hipbones, which had not knitted properly in the plaster shell. Crick-crack went the breaking bones, and Homa fainted. Tears replaced the hammers in Miriam Hanoum's eyes, she rubbed her daughter with egg yolks, turmeric, and cumin, bound her legs with reeds and sheets, and Homa remained in bed until the end of winter.

Ever since then Homa dragged her crippled leg as if it were unwanted, raising a cloud of dust behind her. Her limp kept the suitors away and left her an embittered spinster in her parents' home until she was fourteen, at which time, for want of a better choice, she was betrothed to Mahatab Hanoum's slow skinny son. She used to pound her little sister's blooming rounding body with her hands, which had grown very stout since she became lame. When ragged Hayim the beggar passed their house, Homa would point to him and shout: "Flora, Flora, here comes your bridegroom."

"Not true!" Flora would pout when she had looked through the window.

"It is so true," Homa would reply calmly, studying her fingernails. "He's the father of your babies, go and dress up for him!"

Her mother-in-law, Mahatab Hanoum, had the finest voice in the village. She sang at all the festive gatherings, but only after lengthy and ceremonial urging. Her flesh spread and glowed, because at every celebration, big or small, her hosts would press on her delicacies, wine, and compliments, to make her sweet voice rise from her corpulence up to the stars. One evening she came to the Ratoryan house and kissed every member of the family as if they were her long-lost relatives. In a clear, rhymed song she asked Miriam Hanoum for Flora's hand, while her son, the prospective bridegroom, accompanied her, playing a fractured melody on the flute.

Before she reached the first refrain, Miriam Hanoum pulled the flute from the son's mouth. The languid notes faded in the hashish and opium smoke that hung in the room, and the boy's mouth remained open. He looked up at his mother, his lower lip drooped to his chin, and his mouth arched as his shoulders rose bashfully to his ears. But though the flute fell silent, Mahatab Hanoum, with her eyes shut and her lashes trembling with emotion, went on rhyming Flora's beauty with her son's charms.

"Enough," Miriam Hanoum raised her hand above her head. "We've heard how beautifully you sing." She told the singer she wouldn't give her Flora, who deserved a better bridegroom, but she thought that the match would suit Homa.

"The lame one?" said Mahatab Hanoum.

She examined Homa from top to toe, looked at her son's imbecile expression, and agreed. But since it was not Homa or her limp she had intended for her son, she never missed an opportunity to offend her. She would send her to press grapes for wine and vinegar, pushed her when she was holding pots of hot soup, beat her with fists and sticks, and at festive family gatherings forced her to dance and amuse the guests with her hobbling.

On the morning of the henna feast, a day before the wedding, when the bridegroom's mother puts the bride through the *sabzi* test, to examine her modesty and her quality as a housewife, Mahatab Hanoum's song was so derisive, and her sisters' eyes were so fixed on her crooked leg, that Homa nearly failed.

The bride was expected to display her skills at cleaning and chopping the *sabzi,* the seasoning herbs that Janjan sold in the bazaar. Nazie was nine years old and Flora thirteen when the joyous ululations, *li-li-li,* burst out around Homa, and the bride's kohl–painted eyes widened in alarm. The women of the family and the village formed a circle around her, pressing their breasts together and shaking them as they danced with widespread legs, laughing and beating on drums. Nazie and Flora, barefooted, pushed through the dancers' legs. All the women sniffed with pleasure at the giggling Flora and scolded Nazie for not sprouting breasts. Nazie was as tense as if it was she and not Homa who was going to marry the singer's son. She ignored the teasing and observed everything closely, learning and absorbing, so as not to fail the *sabzi* test when her time came.

Mahatab removed from Homa's shoulders the great chador, which was interwoven with gold and silver threads and fringed with bells, folded it four times, until it fitted

the bride's head. Having tied the shawl-turned-into-a-ker-
chief behind Homa's neck, she tucked her black curls into
it so that they would not cross the boundary of her eyebrows and fall into her eyes. With pale and compressed lips
she kissed Homa on both cheeks, and said in her rich voice
that she wished her success. The women trilled with joy as
she placed a silver tray before the bride, heaped with bundles of celery, tarragon, sage, rosemary, mint, leek, and parsley. Homa sat cross-legged on the floor, and the green
mound of the *sabzi* reached her breasts.

Miriam Hanoum sat beside Homa and rubbed her
back, whispering to her that it was bad enough having a
crooked back and leg, she must not let anxiety twist her
face, too. She observed the level of the green pile, because
if it was too high, it meant that the bridegroom's mother
was unhappy about her daughter-in-law. But Mahatab
Hanoum was fair, and Miriam Hanoum signaled to Homa
to start. Homa nimbly separated the celery stalks from the
leaves and root, the leek stalks from their bulbs, the sage
from its scented buds, and dunked them all in the big bowl
of water. Then she rinsed the mint leaves, the tarragon, and
parsley. When the sand had sunk in the bowl and the *sabzi*
showed bright and green, Homa tore off the limp and yellowing leaves, while the women cheered her on, warbling
songs of encouragement and competition. Homa arranged
the washed herbs in bundles and laid them side by side in
rows. Nazie trembled with fear. She did not take her eyes
off Homa's fingernails. Her stomach muscles clenched, as
though gripping something to stop it falling, and even
Flora choked back her laughter for fear it would break out
and cause Homa to fail.

Homa took the well-honed knife. Its blade flashed, and

the women hushed each other. Nazie knew that the examined brides sometimes cut their fingers in agitation, even cut off a finger, which they gave their mothers to keep and went on with the test, bleeding before time. But if not a single drop of blood fell throughout the test, and in the end the herbs were chopped extremely fine, the women would sing and dance around the bride who had learned the craft so well in her parents' kitchen.

Just before the women began to dance in her honor Homa raised her chin from the herbs to catch her mother's encouraging smile, and the knife nicked the back of her hand. Being accustomed to pain, she bit it back and stirred the blood into the eager green of the herbs. Mahatab Hanoum did not notice the cut, and the few such as Nazie, who did, said nothing. The house filled with loud rejoicing and the fresh fragrance of the herbs, and when these had been thrown into the pot and cooked in oil along with chunks of veal, grains of wheat and slices of beet, and were served to the guests on the henna evening, the beet hid the disgrace of Homa's bleeding.

The following day Homa and the son of Mahatab Hanoum were married, and the bridegroom's consumptive father was breathing his last. His body was even thinner than his son's, and on the eve of the wedding he smelled of garlic, vinegar, and urine. When the festivities ended and the guests left, he was found dead in his chair, his fingers frozen in a drumming movement. Joy turned to mourning, and the tired guests returned from their houses to console Mahatab Hanoum the widowed singer and the new bridegroom. Miriam Hanoum searched everywhere for her daughter, and when at last she found her dragging her leg in one of the alleys, she warned her not to couple with her husband that night, because she was supposed to feel grief, and misplaced lust was bad for any conception, much less the first one. "He's your husband and you will be able to enjoy him all your life. Restrain yourself, Homa, restrain yourself…," she said, because she knew how hot she was.

But when the two lay down at midnight on the coir mattress, Homa forgot her mother's injunction, her husband forgot his father's cooling corpse, and his slender body grew hot between her stout arms. The following morning, when Homa assured her mother that she had obeyed her and that she and her husband had not touched each other, Miriam Hanoum fed her celery, for her children to be healthy, made her drink an infusion of laurel flowers, to make them beautiful, and gave her slices of citron, for their skin to be fine and sweet-smelling. As soon as the dead man was buried, her husband's sharp pelvic bones again bore into Homa's blubber, and she conceived.

Homa writhed in labor for seven whole days, and her husband's sisters said it was her mother's pampering that was holding up the birth. Only on the seventh morning of Homa's screaming did Zuleikha, the deaf midwife, understand that the girl was not spoiled and the baby was not contrary. She stuck her head between Homa's legs and smiled. Homa was a virgin. When she fell with the kite, her hipbones broke and her maidenhead was pushed up toward the womb. Her skinny husband's member never broke it, and the baby had been butting against it in vain for a week. Zuleikha emerged from between Homa's spread thighs and returned with a pair of tiny scissors. When the membrane was cut and its blood stained the sheets, she beamed and said in her thick voice:

"There, Miss Homa, I made you a Missis. Now push and you will be a *kuchik madar.*"

When the baby's head was out of its mother's body, they all saw that its wet face bore an amazing resemblance to his dead grandfather. Like him, he had a round owl's face, his hair grew in a triangle from a bump in the middle of his forehead, and his black eyes were very close together, ringed with light-colored fuzz. Miriam Hanoum went pale with grief and rage. She plucked five hairs from the baby's head, so that the demons would not confuse him with the dead man, and turned to question her daughter.

"It wasn't me, ma, honest, it was him, he touched me first on the wedding night," Homa sobbed, exhausted.

"All right, close your legs," said Miriam Hanoum and covered her with the sheet. She took the owlet from its mother and called in the whole family to bid him good-bye.

"Ma, just let me suckle him. They are bursting with milk," Homa pleaded, holding her swollen breasts. "It hurts."

"No. The grandfather's soul is in the child," said Miriam Hanoum. "He'll die in a few hours and will punish his mother and father." Then she attached a leech to the baby's pink back. When the leech swelled, she removed it, passed a razor over the rounded baby fat, and again attached a leech to the scratched flesh, to draw off the blood with the curse. But the baby died early in the morning. Miriam Hanoum wept, Mahatab Hanoum wept, and so did Manijoun, Flora, and Nazie. Homa squeezed her aching nipples and pressed her nose to the baby and kept sniffing him, because she thought he smelled of garlic.

Homa never conceived again. Miriam Hanoum caught geckos in the village windows and set them loose in the house of Homa and her husband. But the geckos escaped, taking their lucky tails to the neighbors' houses and filling them with children. The women undid their bodices at every whimper, stuffed nipples into mouths, and the warm smell of the milk inflamed Homa's envy. "Homa doesn't think with her head anymore," said Miriam Hanoum sadly. "Now she can only think with her hole, which is burning with grief."

Every spring Moussa would wander off with his white hound in the fields of Omerijan to look for mandrakes. He dug up the man-shaped roots, which had arms, legs, and a head, and brought them to his sister. The heavy scent of their purple flowers with yellow pistils filled the house and intoxicated Homa. But the mandrakes availed nothing, nor did the psalm notes written by rabbi *mullah* Netanel the widower, which Homa swallowed with her meals. In her longing for the dead baby owl, she fed her husband fenugreek seeds, scratched his back with her finger rings, and his thin member did not come out of her body all night long. The cries of lust that rose from her house entertained the entire village and spread lewd smiles on the faces in the Jubareh.

Part Three

THE
WEDDING

CHAPTER FOURTEEN

THAT NIGHT NAZIE DREAMED that Miriam Hanoum was presenting her with a heap of old yellowing *sabzi* with dry and shriveled stems. When she woke at dawn, she was greatly puzzled to see that Flora's bed was empty. The smell of her watermelon vomit still hung in the air, and her dress was thrown on the rug, but her blankets were neatly folded and her sheet was smooth.

Nazie ran barefoot to the privy, to pee and check if she had grown up during the night. On her way there she saw that Flora was not in the house, and when she took off her underpants, there was no trace of blood. Drops of hot urine spattered on her elbow-sharp ankles and her upturned heels. She whispered: *"Farhiz...farhiz...farhiz...,"* to warn the demons to move their tender babies away from the scalding stream.

Returning glumly to the house, Nazie saw Moussa's back, broad as a mattress, curled on the Kashani carpet in a corner of the sitting room. Going back into the girls' room, she thought sadly that she was tarrying while Moussa kept growing all the time and had no time for her.

She felt Flora's stretched bedsheet, her properly folded quilt, and passed her fingers over the cool bedding. Flora must have left the house a long time ago, she thought as she stacked up the mattresses.

First she lighted coals in the brazier, as she did every winter morning. Then she raked the cinders from the stove and added pinecones and the scraped pieces of watermelon shell to its fire. After warming herself at the fire, she went down to the cistern where the water was nearly frozen. Returning to the kitchen, she filled the samovar, cooked eggs, kidney beans, and porridge, and baked flat bread. Having scraped the *gondi* fat from the saucepans with a bald corncob, she quit the sooty kitchen and swept the floors, ejecting into the alley moth corpses and Flora's hairs, which had been torn out in sorrow and formed dust balls in corners and on the rugs.

She heard a mouse slipping out into the alley, stood on tiptoe, and opened the window high above her head. Cold air blew into the stuffy house. Breathing deeply, she watched a solitary bird that twittered on top of an almond tree, and the snow shovelers, early risers like her, sweeping the snow from the roofs.

Ever since her parents died, Nazie rose every morning at dawn and immediately set to work on the household chores, but it was only the odor of the rye bread, which she baked in the late hours of the morning, that broke into Flora's sleep and dragged her from her bed. Even before washing her face in the water butt, while her dreams still lingered in her half-opened eyes, Flora would sip the hot milk and chew on the bread Nazie gave her. She still slept late when she yearned for Shahin, but despair made her slumber lighter. She reacted to every rattle of Nazie's saucepans with an irritable moan and turned on her back. She also complained about the rousing mixtures of spices, saying that their mad odors were bothering her, dispelling the effect of the espand seeds and destroying her rest.

The night before, the strange unpleasant taste of envy, which clung to Nazie's tongue ever since she was taken in by her aunt, had scalded her throat as hot urine scalds the skin of an infant demon. She tried to swallow its bitter taste with her saliva and to put Flora's odd disappearance out of her mind. When she woke Moussa and his father by gently shaking their shoulders, she did not tell them about Flora's empty bed, nor did she mention it afterward, when they sat, washed, and dressed, sipping the black tea she served them. Every morning she looked at the reflection of her face in the teacup before handing it to Moussa and, on Sultana's advice, checked every feature so as to preserve their love. Even when she sat down with them, plaiting her long hair while they fished the fragrant pine needles from their cups and swallowed the remaining tea, Nazie did not recall Flora and did not tell them that she had disappeared.

Moussa stood beside the door, holding his broad-brimmed felt hat—a recent fashion, suggestive of faraway lands beyond the Caspian Sea—and looked at Nazie's little face, her pointed chin and the cheekbones widening above it, like an inverted drop of water. With her eyes lowered, she indicated to him that there was no news between her legs. It struck her that the lemony pimples were multiplying on his face. When he asked if she would be in the market that day and would come to the poultry shop, she replied that she would be there at midday, and thought about Shahnaz Tamizi.

She looked through the window as Moussa walked with

his father out of the alley, and noted sadly how bowed his
strong shoulders were in the morning. Although they ran
the family poultry shop honestly and diligently, they had a
harder time than Rohollah, the butcher whose stall
adjoined theirs. Moussa's father was the fourth in a line of
butchers, but their strange family name—Ratoryan meaning milkman's son—put many customers off. They said
they would rather buy their poultry from a gentile butcher
than from a Jewish one whose name was tainted with
soured milk.

The price of the birds sold by the family decreased from
generation to generation, and only the poor villagers
bought an elderly chicken from them once a fortnight.
Their wives prepared soup for a week from its fatty flesh
and then used it, wrapped in muslin, to enrich their hum-
ble dishes. On other days they bought *dombeh* and feathery
skins, seasoned the fat with cumin and pepper and roasted
it on charcoal, spread it on bread, and stuffed it into their
children's mouths.

Only before Flora's father and brother did they shed
their pride and admit their poverty. They hid their hunger
from their neighbors and pretended to be too full to eat
anything, even when only tea and bread were available.
The women set pots of water to boil with some dill weed,
to make their neighbors believe that they were cooking a
thick *khoresht* soup, and when their children cried for
food, they would pound the pestle in the empty mortar
for the neighbors to think that they were pounding meat
for the midday meal. In the year of the great drought all
the women of the Jubareh pounded air, and the odor of
imaginary *khoresht* rose from all the kitchens.

When Moussa and his father disappeared beyond the

houses of the Jubareh, Nazie quickly undid her plait and loosened the hair on her shoulders. She opened Flora's cosmetics box avidly and powdered herself with its powders. She rubbed three drops of fragrant rose oil on her neck and three more on her face. With untrained fingers, more accustomed to pickling fish and pressing cheese than titivating, she painted her eyelids. She worked quickly, before Miriam Hanoum woke up and caught her in the act. In the weak light from the window the mirror reflected a dim, pallid image, but when she approached the lighted stove, she saw that her face was painted like the faces of the women who stood in the entrance of Mamou's whorehouse, slapping their buttocks and praising their flesh to the men. She licked her thumbs and rubbed her face with them, but the paint smeared and her face looked uglier. Her looks in the mirror frightened her, but Nazie was determined to appear as mature as possible.

She tried on two of Flora's flowered dresses but took them off again and stood naked and perspiring. Finally she decided to wear the full silken dress that Shahin had made for his wife on the eve of their wedding. She tied up its ample folds so that it would not drag on the ground as she walked, and put on Flora's patent-leather high-heeled shoes. But since there was no way to make them fit her feet, and they clattered on the floor, she took them off and put on her plain cloth shoes, which disappeared under the dress. Before leaving the house, she threw a final glance at the queen's sad green eyes. It seemed to her that a subtle smile had appeared overnight between the woven cheeks. Nazie tied her kerchief on her head, glanced at her grand-mother snoring in her crib, and went outside, dragging the white train through the puddles.

Flora had married Shahin on a beautiful spring evening, and her wedding dress, though ample, was light and delicate. Now the fierce winds of early winter whipped it, shook and filled it, and almost threw Nazie to the pavement. Nazie, who always walked carefully and straight, as though someone had drawn a line on the ground for her, stumbled and swayed like a drunkard. She pressed her arms to her sides, not because of the cold, but because she feared that the hem of the dress would fly up and reveal the plain cloth shoes hidden underneath. Despite the early hour and her choice of byways, wherever she went she was followed by astonished looks, loud laughter, and jeers.

The young workmen, thinking they had discovered a new girl, flirted with the strange coquette and approached her, buzzing like bees. When they realized that it was Nazichi Ratoryan dressed like a Gypsy, they became uproarious, trailed after her, and harassed her like gnats. She would have liked to slap them down, but the gnats multiplied and became a swarm of wasps. In the maze of alleys children tried to grab the train of her dress, and she stumbled again and again. Finally she gathered up the mud-laden flounce and with short, quick steps and bowed back ran out of the Jubareh, exposing her cloth shoes for all to see. Pieces of wash tossed about by the winds seemed to her like bodiless people chasing after her.

When she reached the house of *mullah* Hassan, his servants were amused by the sight of the ridiculous child, and one of them asked with a toothless grin: "What happened, Nazichi, you want to be a gentile orphan?" When she said that she needed to see the *mullah* urgently, they told her that he had gone the week before to the holy city of Qom, and would return the following day.

Walking close to the garden walls of the houses, Nazie made her way to the house of the *kadkhoda,* the village head, which stood on the other side of Omerijan. Like her pregnant mother, she circled the perimeter of the village, and her heart trembled with fear. The *kadkhoda's* two wives stood in the doorway, one big and one small, both pregnant, frowning and flaring their nostrils. When Nazie asked to go in and speak to their husband, but would not say what she wanted of him, the smaller wife swept her from the threshold with her prickly twig broom, and the big one chased her as far as the gate, yelling at her never to dare approach the house of a respectable Muslim dressed like a little Jew whore.

By the time she reached the mosque near the market, she was weeping bitterly, her feet hurt, and the rumor had swept over the village that the demons had turned Nazichi Ratoryan into a white dove, but she was unable to fly.

The bazaar was thronging with people carrying baskets, peasants yelling at mules laden with vegetables and fruit, sheep walking calm-eyed to slaughter, dogs fighting over a bone, and cats exploring piles of garbage. The stalls were heaped with immense pumpkins, white cauliflowers like human skulls, cucumbers and carrots as long as the butchers' knives. The odor of barley and rice, which had been cooking all night in tubs, invited the workmen to breakfast. The hard-boiled eggs that had been buried in the porridge emerged looking brown and mottled. Slices of dry cheese and charcoal-roasted beet were sold and devoured in the corners of the square, and everyone talked in awe about Mamou's demon baby with the double genitals and gave thanks that it was dead, clouds of vapor rising from their mouths into the cold air.

The dome of the mosque was perfectly round like a baby's belly with a dagger thrust in its navel. Above it, the wind sent feathery white clouds flying across the sky. The date palms led Nazie to the entrance. Inside the courtyard she was seized by two men, and she screamed and wept, saying that she had to see *mullah* Ja'afar, because only he could save her. Finally they pitied her and agreed to take her to him, but she had to drape a big worn camel-hair chador over her shoulders. For the first time Nazie saw the mosque from inside, its great arches, the carpets on the floors, and the blue tiles on the walls. She waited in a small antechamber, and when they called her in, she trembled all over.

When she entered his room, she saw the *mullah* absorbed in his books. He had on an ascetic's black robe and on his head the white *amameh* bonnet, which looked like half an egg. Flora's wedding gown was wet and muddy, and Nazie's face was smeared with paints. A heavy smell of strange old women's sweat clung to the dusty chador she was wrapped in, overcoming the scent of rose oil. She bowed deeply, greeted the old man politely, and took the kerchief off her head, exposing her hair and her ears, which were burning with shame. Her shoulders rose as if a flock of pigeons were perched on them.

The *mullah* looked up from his books and stared in surprise at the little fledgling of a Jewess standing before him. Hesitant and curious, he put down the prayer stone and the string of amber beads and fingered his graying beard. Without a word, he poured water into a copper bowl and rinsed his hands, sprinkling his fingers, forehead, nose, and bare feet.

Nazie had never seen him before, but she remembered

that every time she picked her nose Miriam Hanoum said that if she did not stop, she would have a huge nose like *mullah* Ja'afar's. When he looked up from the purification bowl, the menacing nose appeared, surmounted by a pair of eyeglasses with thick lenses, through which gazed his kindly eyes that could read the alphabet of the English and decipher the handwriting of the demons.

"Yes, young lady, what do you want from me?" the old man asked, surprising Nazie by the gentleness of his voice.

"I've come to ask for your help, your honor. I'm Nazichi the orph…," she whispered, looking down at the tips of her wet cloth shoes.

"What?" he shouted. "I can't hear you like that. Come closer and speak loud, don't be afraid, young lady, come." When she moved closer, she regretted that she had not worn the high-heeled shoes, because she felt smaller than ever. She knelt at the man's feet, and her knees sank into the pile of the carpet, which had a picture of lions rending deer woven in it. His big nose rose and spread above her, its skin full of black bumps.

"Here, young lady, *befarmai,* please eat something." He offered her almonds and pistachio nuts on a copper platter embossed with pomegranates. The child sitting before him trembled, and her eyes darted from the window to the door and back. Her neck swiveled like a frightened bird's, and there were bluish streaks of tears on her thin face.

"Only you can help me, sir," she said in a piping voice. Then she remembered that she ought to straighten her back and stretch her neck, to fool the old man into thinking that she was older than she was.

"Louder, my child, louder. I can't hear you. I am, as they say, an old mule, and the ears don't hear as well as they used to, and you are a little Jew girl and your mouth is small. How old are you?" He stuck out his chin amiably and a pleasant smile formed in his beard.

"I'm twelve years old, by my God, so help me if I'm lying, sir," she said quickly, and smacked her flat chest as if swearing an oath.

The man sighed. His forehead wrinkled, his nose grew still longer, and his kindly eyes narrowed. The clicking of the amber beads combined with the clatter of the rain on the window. After they had been silent for a little while, Nazie told him haltingly about her parents and Moussa and Miriam Hanoum, and the vow her aunt had made to her dead mother. She also spoke about the people who gossiped about her and Moussa, swallowing the ends of sentences to start new ones. The old man's eyes blinked doubtfully, and the words she had repeated in her mind on her way became scrambled in her mouth. When his pupils disappeared altogether behind his hairy eyelids, she thought he had fallen asleep. The amber beads also fell silent. She wanted to shake him by the shoulders, to pull his nose and scream into his ears to wake up, because she needed him to help her, because she, too, wanted a baby and a watermelon, because if he did not listen to her, then Shahnaz Tamizi and the king's new laws would take Moussa away from her, and she would remain alone, alone, alone.

Nazie knew that before Reza Shah published the new laws, the *kuchik madar* were betrothed in their mothers' bellies, and conceived before their first period. The cemeteries were full of girls who died in childbirth, lying in their small tombs beside their babies who were buried in still smaller graves. In the first proclamation the Minister of

Health announced that a *kuchik madar* could be married only if it was shown that she had reached puberty. When the Shah's councilors realized that his officials and soldiers could hardly probe between the legs of all the girls in the realm, a second, amended proclamation was issued. Marriage was permitted from the age of twelve, provided the girl had reached puberty. Nazie was not yet twelve, and everyone knew she had not yet had a period. She had heard it said that *mullah* Hassan and the *kadkhoda* could be bribed with silver and gold to allow a marriage in violation of the law of the realm, but about *mullah* Ja'afar it was said, with head shaking and compressed lips, that he was honest and strict and hard to tempt.

"And have you already, as they say, become a woman?" The *mullah* surprised her, opening his eyes and revealing their light. Nazie blinked and remained silent, as though considering her reply. Her silence grew long, and the old man stroked his beard, as though seeking to lengthen it, too.

In the first years of the law there were many offenders who married their daughters off in secret. Evading the eyes of the king's officials, the pregnant *kuchik madar* hid at home for nine months, until their shrieks broke through the closed doors. The midwives of Persia stopped taking the women in labor out into the courtyard, despite the ancient belief that a woman who did not expose her pangs to the sunlight would give difficult birth to stubborn and inconstant children, the same as the women who conceived while riding on the husband instead of lying under him. Some midwives substituted tubs of hot water under the woman's buttocks for the sunlight. The fathers who were caught were sent to prison for a hundred days, but the marriages held. Only the sworn testimony of two women who were not related to the family, vouching that they had seen the girl's menstrual blood with their own eyes, could set the father free.

"I understand," the *mullah* interpreted her silence. "And you, as they say, love this Moussa?" he asked.

"He's in my blood, sir, he must not marry another woman. There's a vow. He's like nettles in my soul, sir, he's in the blood…"

"And your life, what is that? Look how small your bones are, how can you give birth with such short bones? And your body is so frail, as if you don't eat at all. They call you Nazie, don't they? Truly, you are as delicate as a bird. Me, if only I could, my child, I would give all my remaining years for a single day from my childhood. And you want to give up your childhood—for what, for gray hair? Gray hair and sorrow in the eyes are not bought in the market, my child. You pay for them with childhood. With childhood. So, what shall we do now? Time, as they say, will make a woman of you. Wait a year or two, grow a little, and with Allah's help…"

"You don't understand, sir, I must now, in the blood…," she went on trying, the words scorching her mouth like glowing embers.

"But there is a law, my child." Abruptly, he raised his voice and added firmly, "And I can't let the law, as they say, be broken." He went on speaking with his eyes shut, as though unwilling to hear any more. Nor did Nazie hear any more. She broke into his speech, and a great desperate voice came from her throat.

"But he's in my blood, sir, like nettles, and the time is

passing and people are saying terrible things…," she said and started to cry, feeling that she had lost the old man's pleasant smile and luminous eyes and that he had closed his face. She no longer looked at him but stared at the ceiling and shouted about honor and shame. Her shouting was heard outside, fetching excited men from the mosque courtyard, who rushed in to save *mullah* Ja'afar from the din that the Jewish girl was raising. Still shouting, Nazie stood up, and the chador slipped from her shoulders. The copper platter was overturned, and the almonds and pistachios cracked under her stamping feet.

Had Nazie contained herself a moment longer, wiped the tears from her eyes, and looked again at the man's face, she would have seen that his old heart had softened and gone out to her. But the room filled with angry men, and Nazie's patience snapped. Wrapping her head in a kerchief before going out into the rain, which sang in the window although the sun had come out, her fingers touched the golden fishes dangling from her ears. The coins tinkled delicately. Nazie grabbed the fishes and tugged hard.

The hooks of the earrings, which Miriam Hanoum had sneaked into the holes years before, cut through the lobes and split them in half. The blood gushed from the flesh and spurted merrily, as though it had been waiting for this moment. The ears competed with one another in spurting as much blood as they could on the big wedding gown. Nazie's face twitched with pain, and she saw great gouts falling on the carpet, bleeding on the bodies of the deer that the lions were tearing apart with their fangs. The men who had seized her arms to drag her outside were shocked and let go. Nazie put the wet earrings in the hand of the *mullah,* who had come up to her in astonishment, and closed his fingers on them. His jaw dropped in alarm, his eyes bulged, and now finally Nazie looked straight at them and asked that in return for the earrings he would grant her wish and allow her to marry her cousin Moussa.

CHAPTER FIFTEEN

Nazie's whispers, *FARHIZ, farhiz*, before falling asleep had availed nothing—the laughing demons sneaked into Flora's belly, pinched the baby's bottom, and pulled his ears. The sharp edge of the knife that Miriam Hanoum had slipped under Flora's pillow when she found that her daughter was pregnant failed to keep the evil spirits away. Nor did the broom of paradise help. The fetus woke its mother from her slumber, and she lay on her back, her eyes open, to watch over it until it settled down and allowed her to sleep.

Little yawns fluttered between her lips, and she pressed her cheek to the pillow and gazed at the brazier through the open door of the room. A few embers still glowed amid the black cinders, and now and then a red tremor ran over them. The scent of rosemary blended with the sour smell of the watermelon vomit. Flora had not taken off her dress, but the ugly juice stains had already dried.

Beside her bed stood the pine cradle that Zuleikha's husband had made for the awaited baby. Flora rocked it, and the new cradle squeaked softly, like a sleeping baby.

The balls of socks, the folded diapers, and the tiny woolen shirt slid from side to side. Through the darkness Flora observed the small mound made by Nazie's body under the woolen blanket, rising and falling as she breathed. Flora thought that if Nazie curled up a little more, she could fit into the cradle as Manijoun fitted into her basket, like an egg in a nest, and Flora could rock her and sing her rude lullabies until she slept.

"Nazie," Flora whispered, rising on her elbows. "Nazie?"

She wanted to say funny things to her until morning, making Nazie stifle her giggles with her hand. Flora could make Nazie laugh till she cried, even without tickling her belly, armpits, or the base of the throat. Once they had both walked barefoot from the marketplace to the Jews' quarter, like a pair of beggar girls, Nazie walking in front with her eyes down, Flora dawdling behind, her eyes raised to the birds. When they reached the synagogue, Nazie stopped, turned around, and shouted at Flora to stop looking at the clouds, because on the ground one can find silver coins that people dropped, or even rings with precious stones, or gold chains that had slipped from their necks.

Something flashed through Flora's eyes. She looked down at the ground, picked up a small stone, and without a thought threw it at one of the synagogue's stained-glass windows. A black hole opened in the colorful pane.

"Flora, what have you done?" Nazie squealed. "Let's go!"

But Flora tiptoed carefully to the wall of the synagogue and cautiously picked up some pieces of glass, red, blue, and yellow, which twinkled in the sun. Nazie giggled and looked around in terror, then followed in Flora's bare footsteps, which turned back to the marketplace and walked confidently to the house of Mamou the whore. Inside the yard, which reeked of urine, Mamou's pampered orphans played at catching carrier pigeons in wicker baskets.

"Don't worry, dopey," whispered Flora, her hands full of shards of glass, to Nazie, who was clinging to her back. "Mamou's orphans open their legs to anyone who passes and they even say 'please.'" She knew that Mamou made a lot of money from the men who visited her whores, and that she indulged all her orphans' wishes, so long as they did not bother her and did what she told them.

Flora pushed her nose between the palings of the whorehouse fence, stuck her tongue out at the girls playing in the yard, and boasted in a childish tone about her treasure. The foundlings pressed against the fence and gazed in wonder at the world through the pieces of colored glass. They saw the crowded marketplace glowing red, blue, and yellow, and Flora sang: "What a beauty, what a color, a lovely city just like abroad!"

They walked home clutching a small coin each, splitting their sides with laughter, Nazie pleading with Flora to stop laughing. She crouched and pressed her hand between her legs, to stop the pee from escaping, but Flora's laughter grew wilder, and she bent down to Nazie's fish earrings and whispered between snorts: "Psss…psss…"

Nazie landed on the path with a bump, and the urine flowed from her laughter, spurting with a hissing sound, wetting her hand and her bare feet. She looked wordlessly at the stain that spread like flowering shame on her dress, and Flora laughed and laughed.

Flora whispered: "Psss…" and smiled to herself. If

Nazie was awake, they would embrace, loosen their hair, and whisper until sleep descended on them from the ceiling. Nazie's triangular face peeped above the blanket, opened like a little fan, her hair tightly braided. Sleep had rolled out the lines in her forehead, the way she rolled out pastry dough. Her lips were open, and the minute coins in the tails of the gold fishes winked at Flora in the dark. She tucked the quilt between her legs and thought about Nazie, her lips, which were always open, day or night, the look in her eyes, which trailed after her thoughts, her fingers, which were forever toying with the fish earrings, sometimes clutching them suddenly, as if someone were after them and wanted to tear them from her ears. She wondered what would have happened if one night her mother pushed her fingers not between her legs, but between little Nazie's legs. What would she have found there? Perhaps Fathaneh was right, and there was nothing there? Or perhaps the opening was too small, and her mother wouldn't have been able to insert a finger?

She heard a distant cry of a strange bird and touched her belly in alarm. In the last few weeks the belly had risen like Nazie's yeast cakes. She thought about their good smell when they rose, plump and brown, when Nazie slid them out of the oven with the flat iron shovel and sprinkled them with melted sugar. Wouldn't it be wonderful if she could turn the rising baby in her belly into flour and oil, yeast and sugar. What a pity that it was not possible to pour the time and Shahin and the baby into the sacks and casks in the larder.

The peculiar idea amused Flora. She grinned in the dark, turned from side to side, and again looked at the brazier, which had turned quite black. She gave up trying to capture evasive sleep, and let go its squirming tail.

Rain beat down angrily on the village roofs, and the wind rattled the windows, loosening the dust in their cracks. Flora got off the bed, and her plump feet sank in the layers of carpets. They only felt the night's chill when she stood in the courtyard beside the water butt, which was full of water and floating feathers, and washed her face. The sound of the door opening and shutting did not interrupt the snores of the family and Manijoun's restless mutterings. When she returned to her room, she folded her bedclothes neatly, took off her stained dress, and rubbed her arms and neck with fragrant rose oil. Then she put on thick stockings and another pair over them, a quilted blue dress with ample sleeves fitted at the wrist, over which she slipped on a pleated gown made of the orange wool of she-camels, then drew on a pair of pantaloons belted with colored ribbons. The mirror showed her how big she was. She looked at her puffy face above the broad shoulders and wrapped it in a white kerchief folded into a triangle. One end hung down on her back, and the other two she knotted under the fat folds of her chin. The hanging ends rose and fell on her breasts. Finally she encased herself in the great chador, which fell down to her legs, pulled it tight around her ears and went out into the street to look for her lost sleep.

"Where are you going in your dreams, bad girl?" Manijoun rose from her basket. Her ancient eyes closed again, but her mouth remained open.

"Shhh...," whispered Flora with a finger to her lips, her head inside the house and her body already out of it. "Sleep, Grandma, sleep."

"Mustn't go out now, bad girl, go back to your dreams. You mustn't." Flora heard the old woman muttering as she softly closed the door.

The darkness and the hour felt strange to her. The familiar village had turned quite black. The skyline of roofs and treetops was obscured, and the face of the village sank like that of an old man. The wind fluttered the chador around her head and tore her hair loose, making it flutter like a flag on the pole of her body. When she emerged from the alleys of the Jubareh, strange dogs barked at her, then stopped after she passed, and listened to the echo of their barking following her echoing footsteps. Reaching the marketplace, she stopped beside the fence of the lighted, crowded whorehouse and listened to the men's hiccups and the women's laughter. Suddenly she felt very thirsty. Like a sleepwalker, she entered the *kahweh khooneh,* the coffeehouse next to Mamou's place, that was painted bright blue all over.

She used to peer curiously into its interior and watch the red-eyed men playing chess and backgammon, swearing and singing lewd songs, dragging the pieces, and slamming them hard on the wooden boards. Mamou's customers, after leaving her house and pissing in her yard, would tie their trousers, spit at the corner, and harass the women shoppers in the market. Seeing Flora staring at them big-eyed, they would invite her to join them in the coffeehouse. But Nazie would tug at her dress in fright and pleadingly drag her away.

Flora walked into the lighted billows of smoke, her eyes half shut like a somnambulist, and passed between the oil lamps. At once the eyes of the drugged men, their hoarse laughter and lewd jokes, were drawn to her full breasts, her backside, and belly. They uttered sharp whistles of admiration under their curling mustaches, but Flora did not turn back, because good little Nazie was not behind her, pulling at her kerchief and imploring tearfully, "Enough, Flora, come on out." She was not afraid, because she knew that Moussa and his dog were asleep and would not be looking for her. Shahin, too, was gone and was not there to reach for her nightgown, feel its rustling fabric, and tuck his head between her breasts.

From the depths of the den men crept toward Flora, putting out long writhing arms, their eyes rolling to the ceiling, whispering together with mouths that reeked of hashish and opium and rotten teeth.

"Miss Flora," they buzzed and chirped, "couldn't you fall asleep this black night?"

"Too hot to sleep tonight, eh, Miss Flora, time to celebrate…"

"Are you cold, Miss Flora, you want us to hug you and stroke you and set your pretty body on fire?"

"This isn't a body for sleeping, Flora, it's a body for partying…What's the matter with you, what are you afraid of?"

Hairy paws multiplied, reaching for her breasts, her buttocks, and belly, hovering over her sleepy indifference. Yellowed fingers scratched her skin, lustful hands slapped her flesh, her dresses rustled one on top of the other, and the men grew merrier.

"My teeth…," Flora mumbled dully. "Teeth hurt." She pressed her hand to her round cheek, to show that she was in pain.

The men crowed delightedly as if her teeth were a gift from heaven. They spat on the filthy floor, dipped their black-nailed thumbs in the arrack bottles, and pushed them into her mouth to suck for relief. When, after sucking their fingers, she said she was still in pain, they slid the stone cover off one of the opium pits in the coffeehouse floor.

Flora watched the man who crouched over the little pit and kindled the black lumps for her, and did not struggle when he rose and urged her to kneel and breathe the smoke. Her arms hanging at her side, her knees apart, she submitted to the heavy hand pressing her head down and obeyed the strange harsh voice ordering her to fill her lungs with the smoke. She hoped to find in the cavity the sleep that she and her baby had lost, and her eyelids grew heavy. Intense heat spread in pleasant waves from her womb throughout her body, as if she had mated with the sun and a tiny sun, round and summery, were glowing inside her. She broke out in a sweat and sighed. After a little while she realized that the heat that was spreading soft flames through her came not from the smoke, but from the organ of the man who had lighted the opium for her, and who was pushing her from behind.

Her skirts were up above her waist, and her bottom was bare, shining in the dim light of the coffeehouse. The man had shoved his knees between her thighs, clasped her waist, and with strong rhythmic movements thrust toward her womb. Flora's mind cleared, and she jumped up in alarm, throwing off the man with his member, who slid down without a protest and rolled on the floor. She rallied her melting limbs and, though drained of strength, fled into the darkness.

Flora ran and ran toward the Jubareh without looking back, passed the almond grove, and left the village through the Jews' gate. Only when the night sounds of Omerijan had been left behind her, and all around her stretched open black spaces, did she slow down and stand still, panting and shivering.

The sky shimmered with stars without so much as a sliver of a moon to outshine them, and even the clouds could not suppress their twinkling. Flora decided to keep going. Adjusting the chador on her head, she went on without turning to look at the sleeping village and the wind that trailed behind her. Heavy and quiet, she walked down the wide donkey track, and as she walked, she began to feel better. The wind behind her abated, and with it the intermittent prickly shower. Silvery mists rose like smoke from the ground and drifted around the tree trunks, muddy streams flowed down the hillsides, beads of moisture shivered on the grass. The smell of the watermelon vomit evaporated, together with the scent of rose oil. Only her own sweet sweat accompanied her on her way.

✻ ✻ ✻

At the black mouth of a cave with a spring bubbling out of it, she knelt down for a drink of water. The breaking dawn turned the rocks of the cave blue and the spring water green. A flock of birds flew from the mountains toward the sea. Flora yawned and looked at the emerging outline of the town of Julfah and the villages surrounding it, where early chimneys were beginning to smoke. Between her and the town lay fields of opium poppies, rice, beans, and wheat, melon patches dotted with tiny yellow specks, and blue ponds alive with sweet white fish.

CHAPTER SIXTEEN

WHEN FLORA REACHED THE busy marketplace of Julfah later that morning, she was blue from the cold and her knees trembled with pain. Her shoes were black with mud, and her waterlogged dresses clung to her body, making her swollen belly stick out. But no one took any notice of her.

Strangers walked around her, monkeys danced to their trainers' drumming, snakes rising from baskets swayed to the sounds of flutes. A peddler tried to sell her a bunch of bananas. Flora put out her hand to pluck the yellow fruit, then recalled that she had not brought any money. A dentist invited her to sit in his treatment chair. Beside it was a small table displaying sets of false teeth in pinkish gums. A customer who had just had three of his front teeth pulled out stood up from the chair and opened his mouth wide for the crowd of curious onlookers, who poked fingers into it admiringly. Flora declined to sit in the chair and walked away with the dispersing crowd. The dentist trilled a sad song about a prince whose teeth hurt and who suffered dreadfully, until he found relief in the treatment chair.

Flora stepped aside for a line of creaking handcarts, then made her way to a coach parked on the rim of the sunken square, attracted by the cries of the coachman: "Babol Sar! Babol Sar!" He cupped his hands at his mouth like a trumpet and, when he lowered them, revealed a pencil-line mustache. His eyebrows resembled a pair of scrubbing brushes.

Flora fell at his feet, spattering mud in her eyes and hair, and at once a crowd gathered around her. The coachman, who had seen her coming, put the trumpet back to his mouth and shouted: "Midwife! Midwife!" Three men carried Flora in a large wicker basket to the side of the square, thick veins bulging on their foreheads and necks from the strain.

Despite the old saying that warns against calling in more than one midwife—"A baby pulled by two midwives will have its head torn off"—two of them arrived at the Julfah marketplace, met on the rim, and began to argue who had got there first. Very soon they raised their hands to pull and bared their teeth to bite. Flora rose laughing from the basket and told them that they were both too early. The coachman settled her in the coach, covered her with a plaid blanket from one of the horses, and gave her hot tea and a round Barbary loaf with black olives.

"*Vavaila!* How you run around like this in the rain, with your belly hanging out!" the disappointed midwives scolded the pregnant stranger, shaking their fingers in her face, and warned her that her baby would be sickly and suffer from colds all his life. Flora in alarm swallowed an olive with its pit and laid her hands on her belly to protect Shahin's son from the evil predictions. The midwives went home, the crowd went back to its own business, and the passengers for Babol Sar squeezed into the coach beside Flora.

"You getting off, lady?" asked the coachman, taking up the reins, and his eyebrow-brushes rose to his hairline.

"Can I come too?" Flora asked.

The man looked at her pityingly, scratched his head, shrugged, and whipped up the horses. Throughout the journey to the coastal town of Babol Sar, Flora swayed from side to side between the passengers, huge and laughing.

It was along this route that Flora and Shahin had journeyed on their honeymoon—from Omerijan to Julfah, from Julfah to Babol, and thence to Babol Sar. The vineyards and tobacco fields reminded Flora of her husband's kisses and caressing hands. When they were leaving the village, Moussa had scolded her for giggling: "You're laughing again? What's so funny now? You should cry, not laugh, when you leave home. They'll say you were miserable at your mother's house, that's why you're laughing. Idiot." But Flora clung to her husband's small body and continued to laugh, until she snorted and fell silent.

Shahin led her to a hotel that had sunflower wallpaper on its walls. There he left her alone in a room overlooking the sea and returned late that night, swearing and muttering in Armenian. Flora wanted to spread the sheet with the hummingbirds that Nazie had embroidered for her, but Shahin threw her on her back and entered her, with only the prickly woolen blanket under them. Then they drank wine and arrack, distilled by the landlady in the hotel cellar, and Flora laughed all night. A little before dawn Shahin told her to get dressed and took her to the seashore.

The moon above was silvery and round as their two

faces. "Look what's happening to it, Shahin!" Flora shouted between her husband's arms. When the moon was quite overcome by the black shadow, it swelled and gave off a reddish glow.

At lunchtime they went to a restaurant that had a channel of seawater running through it, and mattresses strewn amid beds of immense roses. Shahin sprawled on a blood-and-grease-stained mattress, and Flora reclined on the cushions at his side. The landlord served them sweetened rose water and slaughtered a tender lamb before their eyes. They remained in the restaurant until nightfall, eating more and more of the roasted lamb, dozing in the pleasant sea breeze, and smelling the fragrant roses. When the sun went down, the landlord came out of the kitchen and announced that there was nothing left but the bones. Shahin told him to make soup with them.

When they returned to their hotel room in the dark, Flora was bursting with stories to tell Nazie, Homa, and her mother. That night she learned that her husband could not fall asleep without rubbing some fabric between his fingers and making it rustle. He rubbed her fine night-gown, and its rustling stopped only when he dozed off. He slept on his left side during the first half of the night, to rest his liver, then woke and turned on his right, to give his intestines a rest.

During the coach ride Flora also remembered bald Morteza Kachalu, who used to live in Omerijan but moved with his parents to Babol Sar. She knew that if Morteza were married, his wife was sure to have thick, long, and silky hair.

Ten carrier pigeons flew to heaven on the day Flora got her first period. The bleeding began at midday, but only at night did Flora discover the darkening streaks that had run down her legs and dried on her ankles. She followed their trail as one follows a snail's track, until she reached the sticky opening. Laughing heartily, she told her secret to Nazie, who told Moussa, who told Homa, who told her father, who told Miriam Hanoum, who proudly informed the whole village. The following day she presented her daughter with a deep bowl full of olive oil, to look at her reflection and see that she was a woman, and asked Nazie to start stitching Flora's bridal sheet.

Nazie worked at it for two years. Every evening she would scrub her housework-grimy hands with lemon halves, to remove the dark grease. When the lemons had turned gray and her clean skin showed, she would pick up the cotton sheet and continue the stitching precisely where she had left off the previous evening. Around the edges she embroidered pairs of courting hummingbirds, their wings outspread and beaks gaping in delight, the males blue and the females purple. Nazie worked patiently and carefully, her eyes always on the sharp point, to make sure she did not prick her finger and allow her virginal blood to stain the needlework. Flora would lie on the rug at her feet, tickle them with a goose feather and dream about the man who would make love to her and the blue and purple hummingbirds.

When they returned from their honeymoon, and Miriam Hanoum asked her laughing daughter to show her the blood flower that had blossomed in the embroidered sheet, Flora slapped her forehead—she had forgotten her bridal sheet in the hotel in Babol Sar.

Flora was eleven when her proud father climbed on Sultana Zafarollah's roof and sent out the news of her nubility to the matchmakers of the surrounding villages, attached to the feet of ten carrier pigeons. After the weary pigeons returned to their dovecot, young bachelors arrived with their old mothers, as well as desperate widowers and men seeking a second wife. They all came to see who was this Flora Ratoryan, whose father averred that she was "beautiful as lemon blossom, smiling like a baby camel, and possessing a good dowry—all assuring a man's happiness." He also wrote that Flora was as sturdy as her mother and older sister, and had recovered from all her childhood ailments as if they were no worse than a mild autumn cold.

"I am certain," he wrote in curling Persian script using a raven's feather dipped in india ink, "that Flora, like her mother, will bear healthy children in exemplary calm without screaming," and sealed the notes with red sealing wax.

The pilgrimage to Omerijan was large and persistent, and the house buzzed with aspiring bridegrooms. Manijoun's basket was moved to the shed, Nazie labored endlessly in the kitchen, and Miriam Hanoum, dressed in her finest gowns, received the would-be grooms and invited them to eat. Her husband would pour the tea and light the hookah for smoking hashish and opium.

When the prospective groom had presented himself, his attributes, and property, Moussa would go with his dog to look for Flora, at Homa's or in the neighbors' kitchens. Sometimes, when Moussa took too long to locate his sister, the suitors would fall for Nazie's cooking, their hearts captivated by her diligence, and they would ask Miriam Hanoum if they could have the younger daughter. Miriam Hanoum decided to lock Nazie in the bean shed, so that she would not disturb the matchmaking. One evening she forgot to let her out, and in the morning Nazie came out soaked in the urine she had been unable to contain, her hands bleeding from her battles with rats.

Miriam Hanoum and her husband chose the richest suitor, bald Morteza Kachalu, whom Flora had known in her childhood. He had become bald at the age of eight. He suffered from ringworm, and his mother took him to the ringworm healer. The heavy-handed woman shaved the boy's head with a razor, smeared his naked skull with warm tar mixed with burnt cow's dung, and bound up the mess with a piece of sackcloth. Morteza wore this heavy cap for three weeks, feeling his scalp burning and his head spinning. On the day he was due to return to the healer, his mother took him to the *hammam,* allowed him to play to his heart's content in the warm pool, bought him a glass of cool *faloudeh* and a bowl of date porridge.

"Finish it now," she said to the healer that evening. "I can't bear to see the boy like this."

She gripped him between her knees, covered her eyes with one hand, and pushed the other one, clenched, into his mouth. Morteza shrieked and bit his mother's fingers, but she held on. The healer took hold of the helmet, which had been softened by the vapors of the *hammam,* and pulled it off his head, and with it, the affected skin and all his hair. When Morteza was twelve years old, a fine mustache appeared on his upper lip, cheering the melancholy boy, who shaved it every day until it thickened. His parents left Omerijan after he went bald, and established a glass factory in Babol, and by the time he returned to the village to ask for Flora's hand, his black mustache was as thick and stiff as that of the king's son, his bald pate gleaming above it. Flora ran to the kitchen and peered through the

open door, laughing and snorting. Her laughter reminded
Morteza of their childhood games. He cast longing glances
at her, puffed out smoke rings, and twirled his mustache.

Miriam Hanoum came into the kitchen, sweeping
Flora before her, and whispered thunderously: "Flora!
Beterki, you should burst! There's a bridegroom in the
house—how long can a bridegroom wait for his bride to
come in?"

"Ma, ma," Flora whined, her ear caught between her
mother's pinching fingers, "I don't want to marry him, he
has no hair."

"*Na kon,* don't be like that, how you talk! He'll get
away, you fool…Well, do you think I wanted to marry
your father?" Miriam Hanoum scolded her daughter and
suddenly chuckled. "Hair's not what matters, you dope.
You'll grow your own hair and he'll bring the money for
you to curl it and put on it flowers and butterflies and hats
with grapes on them. You hear me? Now come inside."

"But ma, ma…"

"Shut up, Flora. I'm going back in there like a bride's
mother, and you come in after me, holding the tray carefully so you don't drop the lemonade, like a good hardworking bride, and bring some seeds, too. And don't laugh
too much, Flora, you hear? You hear me?"

Miriam Hanoum returned to the guests, smiling an
apologetic hostess smile, followed by Flora who was holding back her laughter. She knelt on the carpet and set
down the copper tray, on which rattled the jug with the
juice and the lemon halves and the gold-rimmed glasses.
Flora stood up before Morteza, hands on hips, presenting
herself to his avid eyes, and said in a sweet voice: "I'll just
get some seeds and come back, all right?"

His eyes glittered, and she tripped lightly to the bead curtain. In the kitchen she took a handful of the sunflower seeds Nazie had heaped on a plate, picked up her chador, and said, before slipping out of the house: "He probably stuffs himself with halva, this Kachalu, that's why he has no hair. I don't want him at all."

Moussa found Flora spitting out seed shells in one of the alleys and brought her back. Miriam Hanoum smashed the lemonade jug and fell on her daughter in a rage, dragging her behind the bead curtain. Not wanting the guests to hear blows coming from the kitchen, she silently bit each of Flora's ten fingers, then brought her and the plate with the seeds back to the sitting room.

In the evening Morteza and Flora went for a walk in the village. Flora kept quiet, toying with a flowered handkerchief that she wound tight around her bitten fingers until the marks of Miriam Hanoum's teeth turned yellow. Morteza stopped and begged her to take the kerchief off her head and loosen her hair, as she had done when they were children. Blinking like an owl, compressing her lips into a thin line, Flora freed her hair and let it fall on her shoulders. Now she held a handkerchief in each hand, a flowered one and a gold-threaded one.

Morteza raised his hands to her head, caressed it gently and sank his fingers into the thick hair. For a long time he circled Flora and silently fingered her hair, curled it, softly scratched her scalp, and all the while his mustache tickled her ears and cheeks. Finally he sighed with relief and took her back to her parents' house.

A blazing summer's day followed. "Flora, get up, come on," Nazie shook her excitedly. "You don't know what you're missing, must be somebody dead, there's an enormous funeral." She did not stop until Flora rose sleepily, put on her slippers, and stuck her head through the open front door. A long procession of men and donkeys laden with baskets straggled through the alley. It was led by three musicians—a drummer, a bell ringer, and a flutist. The procession was followed by the neighbors and their children and all the hungry village beggars, shouting and pointing at the Ratoryan house.

One by one, the porters laid the baskets of plenty before the house door and held up long wooden trays. On one tray were red apples wrapped in gilt paper, on another yellow apples with silver ribbons, others held cucumbers, melons, dates, dried apricots, and figs. The baskets overflowed with pistachio nuts, almonds, nutty sweetmeats, sugared peanuts, honeycombs, jars of jam, bottles of wine, various fresh pastries, dry biscuits, and crisp bread. The village poor and the children stared at the abundance of sweet foods, but did not dare to snatch anything.

The bell ringer, a tired little clerical-looking man, whom Nazie and Flora had never seen before, asked everyone to be quiet, signaled to the other musicians to stop playing, and asked which of the girls was the honorable lady Flora Ratoryan. Flora laughed and pointed at Nazie. An astounded murmur passed through the audience.

"What are you doing?" whispered Nazie in fright.

"Don't be an idiot, Flora," said Flora in a loud voice. "Don't you want flowers and butterflies in your hair?"

The man smiled at them, happy to have found the girl at last, because the trek to her house had been long and arduous. He did not notice Nazie's scared expression or hear her mumbled protests. He stuck the bell in his cummerbund, wiped the sweat from his forehead, and said: "I have been sent on behalf of Mr. Morteza Kachalu of Babol. He wishes to say that he remembers from his childhood that the lady likes sweetmeats and fruit, and he urges her to sweeten the fine hours until he returns this evening to the village, to ask her parents to hold the wedding at the end of this week, because his love is pressing."

"Where must I put the presents, Miss Flora?" he asked Nazie when he had finished his speech. Flora stopped laughing, laid an apologetic hand on her nose, which went on snorting, and said: "Excuse us, sir. My sister Flora is a little excited about the beautiful gifts of Mr. Morteza Kachalu, and she asks you to distribute his sweet presents to the hungry and the children."

With a shout, the crowd broke through the line of porters and donkeys standing in the sun, fell like locusts on the food, tore the baskets, overturned the wooden trays, and scattered the delicacies on the paving stones. The little man pulled out his bell and rang it vigorously, but his men were unable to drive back the jubilant crowd and protect the bounty. Faces were smeared with jam, children filled their clothes with sweets, and Flora laughed like a madwoman. The following day the bell ringer returned, this time without a procession and musical instruments, and informed Flora's father that Morteza would not marry his daughter, because his honor had been slighted. Since that time, his mustache and bald pate were never again seen in his native village.

CHAPTER SEVENTEEN

As Flora alighted from the coach in Babol Sar, evening, too, descended on the town. The air was damp and sharp-smelling. Flora was exhausted, and so was the coachman. Tiredness made him impatient, and he put the trumpet of his palms to his pencil line and shouted for passengers to Julfah.

When Flora asked him, between the little ivory yawns escaping from her mouth, if he knew of a hotel that overlooked the sea, had a lot of arrack in the cellar and sunflower wallpaper, the man again looked at her pityingly, and shrugged his shoulders. He thought that he ought to take her back to the marketplace in Julfah, but Flora walked away, still draped in the plaid horse blanket.

Local people directed her to the seashore, to the row of hotels on the front, and warned her against thieves and pickpockets. She followed their pointing fingers, walking hunched against the sea wind, which was blowing in her face, cracking her dry lips and scratching her eyes. Keeping her eyes half shut, all she saw through the thick curtain of lashes were small children, cats, and beggars.

Her thoughts kept returning to the bald head of kindly

Morteza Kachalu, who had lavished fruit and sweets on her, and in return wanted only to play with her hair. Flora thought about his happy, thick-haired wife, whose bald husband loves her and does not abandon her with a baby in her belly and lice in her hair. Every step she took made her belly and breasts bounce, and the sweaty tussling of the three great balls of flesh wearied her. She would have liked to rest, but her belly hurried on. She hung back, but the baby leapt toward his father. In place of the childish courage that had accompanied her, hand in hand, all the way to Babol Sar, shame suddenly overpowered her. And the shame did not come alone—with it came her mother, cursing and swearing with blazing eyes, her father looking strange with his mustache shaved off, Moussa carrying Manijoun in her basket, followed by his slavering white hound, Nazie walking with her eyes lowered, Homa limping after her husband, swinging her massive arms, Homa's mother-in-law Mahatab Hanoum, Sabiya Mansour, Fathaneh Delkasht and her sister Sultana Zafarollah, and all the villagers with their dirty clothes, ugly faces, and barefoot children. They were all chasing after her, shaking sticks and yelling about honor and shame. Flora turned around and gathered her skirts, poised for flight, but there were only small children, cats, and beggars walking behind her.

Breathing heavily, Flora reined in her rushing belly and saw a circle of boys of about her age. She pushed in among them, as if she were one of the gang, and saw in their midst a younger boy, pallid, scrawny, and small. He was wearing a big woman's dress which the boys pulled up, to reveal that he had on a baby's diaper between his legs. The boys were pointing at his loins and singing mockingly: "He's been trimmed! He's been trimmed! He's been trimmed in front!" Flora extricated herself from the ring of boys and went on walking, wearily and clumsily. For a moment it seemed to her that the boys were singing "Flora the whora…," and she wanted to cry like the boy trapped in the circle. A man who was pissing against a wall smiled at her, showing his rotten teeth and shaking his member.

Flora walked past the pissing man and past a lamp-lighter, who was walking from one streetlamp to the next, filling them with oil and lighting them, illuminating her way to the row of hotels, which was lined with carob trees whose sharp odor struck her nose like the smell of Shahin's semen.

There on the seafront stood the hotel, exactly as Flora remembered it. Salty tongues of foam licked the stones, which were coated with a soft velvety green mold. Fishing nets lay in tangled heaps beside the door, and a seagull circled screaming overhead. The sky was the same as it had been, but lacked a moon.

The landlady opened the door. A short woman with a short temper, she was holding an earthen lamp that lit the black moles standing out on her face. Her tired scowling glance swept over Flora's body, from belly to breasts, from chin to eyes, and Flora almost fell into her arms like a long-lost relative. The woman moved back uneasily, fingering the moles on her chin. Then she stepped forward cautiously and raised the light to the big girl's face. The sea breeze blew out the flame, and Flora giggled.

The woman went back into the dark house, relit the wick, and threw shadows on the sunflower wall. The light revealed hairs growing from her moles and blue rings around her eyes. "Come in, come in, lady," she shouted. "The wind's blowing, it'll blow out my brazier, too.

What's the matter with you, why're you standing out there laughing?"

"Thank you, madam, thank you," Flora whispered. The sunflowers looked back at her from all the walls, their dark eyes winking at her from their yellow crowns.

"Why're you standing there like a stick? D'you have any money?" the woman went on shouting, wondering if Flora was deaf or drunk. "I've only got two unoccupied rooms without heat—you want them, take them—if you don't, go to the old Kurd, he's sure to find room for you in his stable."

"No, please listen to me, please listen…" Flora clenched her chattering teeth and whispered quickly: "I'm looking for my husband…" The scowling landlady's eyebrows rose doubtfully. "We stayed here some time ago, in the early spring, to be exact…" She smiled apologetically and laid her hands on her belly.

"*Mobaraket bashi,* congratulations. So what do you want from me, lady?" Flora remembered that in the spring the landlady had been hospitable and generous. She treated Shahin like a relative, told him dirty jokes in Armenian, and filled him up with arrack. Her weary face confused Flora. She stammered and bit her tongue and could not explain what she was hoping to find in her house.

"What did you drink, lady, huh? D'you have any money, or you want to stand here all night telling me stories? I don't have time for this stuff. It's money or good-bye. Go to the old Kurd, maybe he's got some pity left for poor children like you," she grumbled and pushed Flora out of the house.

Flora shook the door with her fists and shouted at the top of her voice: "Open up! *Hoy hoy!* D'you hear me?

Open the door! *Hoy hoy!* You must open for me, please, please, please!" She sank slowly to her knees, her eyes full of tears, and scratched the wood with her fingernails. Sharp splinters stuck in her flesh, and her voice rose till it squeaked: "You must tell me where he is, *hoy hoy!* Open now, it's night, and Shahin…I can't find my husband, he said he was coming back, I swear, so help me, that's what he said, Shahin, my husband. How could you forget so soon? How is it you don't remember, huh? We were here on our honeymoon, Shahin sells silk cloth, and he has a donkey with patches around its eyes, and he, Shahin, my husband, his left eye is a little weak, you forgot? How is it you don't remember? Please open, please, please!"

After a few minutes of silence the landlady opened the door slightly, pushing it against Flora, who was clinging to the wooden panel imploringly with broken nails. The two women peered at each other through the crack. The landlady squinted one eye in a dubious wink and asked slowly: "A weak left eye, you said, weak?"

Flora swallowed nervously. "Hmmm…It's lazy, my husband's left eye. Well, not just weak, lazy."

"No," the woman closed her eyes decisively. "I know one Shahin, don't know his family name or where he comes from, probably from the mountains. But he sells linen, not silk, and he lives not far from here, with the Baha'is, but it must be somebody else, 'cause he's walleyed, really walleyed, in his left eye…"

"Walleyed! Right, right, he's really walleyed!" Flora shrieked and leapt to her feet, forgetting the great belly which curved before her. "Walleyed in his left eye, that's him, yes, where did you say he lives? Here in Babol Sar? Not far?"

"Yes, child, yes, he's Baboli, isn't he? And you say you're his wife? That I can't understand at all…Where did you come from with what you've got in your belly, you poor girl?" Her eyes boded no good, and a trace of doubt lingered in her voice, but Flora did not notice. She felt Shahin's hands peeling the wet dresses from her body, caressing her shivering skin, cradling her butter breasts, relieving her body of all its thick, sweet milk, emptying it of all its sorrow and longings, until she was once again as light and happy as she used to be. She did not feel the intense cold that blew from the sea and shook the carob trees, was not deterred by the sudden downpour that fell on the town, nor did she wonder why the irritable woman had been overcome with compassion and invited Flora to come into her house, to eat and rest and look for Shahin the following day. Flora, weeping and hearing only her own beating heart, begged to be told where her husband lived, and ran to him.

CHAPTER EIGHTEEN

THE CLOSER SHE DREW TO the Baha'i house, the faster beat the tambours in her chest. By the time she reached the handsome two-storied house, set in an orchard of pistachio trees, the drummers were thumping frantically.

Fear brushed her back, crept along her backbone, flickered on her nape, and thrust its slimy tongue into her ears. To expel it, Flora shut her eyes tight and tried to remember Shahin, but the sly demons of Omerijan, who had followed her to Babol Sar, erased the memory of his face, leaving only his hairy, evasive arms. She was tired. She pinched her big cheeks to redden them and shook out her wet hair.

A low stone wall surrounded the orchard, encircled by a fresh-water channel on which floated blackened windfall pistachio fruit. Flora opened the gate cautiously and was greeted by the happy braying of Shahin's donkey, which was tethered to a tree, its coat glistening in the rain. She looked up at the arched windows with little open balconies that overlooked the orchard. Her eyes caressed the colorful mosaic of shells on either side of the door and stared at the stuffed fish set above the doorway, at its glazed eyes and gaping, saw-toothed jaws.

She knocked on the door. No answer. She banged on it hard with her fist and heard wooden clogs clattering inside. A slim woman in a white silk gown opened the door, holding an oil lamp in her delicate hands, which were tattooed with blue and green snakes down to the pale fingertips. Flora's eyes descended from the snake tattoos to the Baha'i woman's belly in its silk drapery, which fluttered in the wind. The slim woman was pregnant. Her hair was the color of milk, and her teeth were small, white, and regular, like the string of pearls around her pale neck.

"What are you looking for, girl?" the woman asked in a voice as thin as her body, and shaded her eyes with her snake-ornamented hand. Flora gazed at her admiringly and said nothing. The woman drew her inside and closed the door, fearful of the wind.

The entrance hall was high and marble-floored, with an empty fountain in its center. Beside the stove stood a round marble table with a carved pedestal, its top inlaid with a black-and-white checkerboard on which were clustered chess pieces. Heavy velvet armchairs surrounded the table, awaiting the players who had abandoned the game and gone about their business. Flora looked at the stairs leading up to the balconied story lit by little oil lamps on the treads. The baby smelled his father and butted and kicked Flora joyously.

"Uh, *bebakhshid,* forgive me, I've come to Shahin, I'm looking for Shahin, his donkey is outside, he's here, isn't he? I saw his donkey outside so I came in, excuse me for coming in like this...You know him, don't you?"

"Yes, girl, of course I know him. I'm his wife, who are you?"

At that moment Flora knew that it was not his father

194

that the vigorously kicking baby recognized, but his brother, and that they were both short-legged like their father. The clothes were bursting on her body.

"Who are you?" the woman repeated. The words in Flora's mouth felt as hard as rocks. She walked over them as on a rugged track and suddenly stumbled and shrieked at the staircase: "Shahin! Shahin! Come here, Shahin! Come down now! It's me, Flora!…What have you done to me, Shahin? What have you done to me? Who is this woman? What's she talking about? Shahin!" Her shrieks sought to mount the stairs, but the slender woman overtook her and barred her way.

"God almighty, girl, what's the matter with you, who are you, anyway? Are you crazy, or what? This is my house! Where did you come from—from hell?" the snake woman cried, her arms crossed to form a single winding snake, her clogs stamping on the marble floor.

"Don't you dare talk to me, *seliteh!* You little Baha'i whore, be quiet!" Taken aback by the Baha'i woman's shouts, Flora spat on her silk-gowned belly.

A tall, long-armed manservant came to the woman's aid, grabbed Flora by the hair, and threw her out. Flora stretched her neck to the balconies and shouted to her husband to show himself at a window:

"Shahin! Who is this woman, Shahin? Come here, tell her that I'm your wife Flora, come, let's go home, Shahin! Oh God, what will I do now? Shahin, come see your poor Flora. Who is this *seliteh* who says she's your wife? Her body should fill with pus, nothing but pus in all her body, yellow, yellow pus…"

She flung stones and sand at the stuffed fish above her and howled at the closed door:

"Who are you, anyway? What d'you want from my husband? Where did you get to know him? Just 'cause he gave you a baby you think you know him? I'm his wife, you hear? And you're just a little *seliteh!* He said he loves me, loves the way my backside moves when I walk…" Flora burst into tears. "He said I was sweet and wet like a goose, when he gave me our baby he said that I was his girl, that I gave him a fever, you hear? A feee-ver!"

Flora fell silent, slumped on the ground with her head on the doorstep, and the donkey stopped braying, too. It looked at her sadly, the white patches around its eyes gleaming like lanterns in the dark. She wept softly and pushed through the crack under the door small stones and curses learned from her mother:

"You should catch all the diseases in the world…You should beg death to come and it won't come, you whore…You should be always too hungry to sleep…You should give birth to a pink monster with five legs and a hump, so you should, *seliteh…*"

From behind her came the voice of Shahin, sniffing at her in astonishment: "Flora? Flora, is that you?"

Butter melted through her body, her face softened, the stones dropped from her hands, and thick, plump tears ran down her cheeks. Snuffling, she asked in a sweet voice, "Shahin, my soul, where have you been?"—as though he had disappeared the day before. His walleye twitched nervously, which Flora interpreted as tears of love. She rose and flung herself, her baby, and the plaid horse blanket into his tense arms, muttering his name eagerly, her nose pecking at his flesh. She was disheveled and warm and wanted him to play with her loosened hair, undo the knots, catch the lice, massage her scalp, and mutter sweet words into her ear, and then her hair would once again be thick and glossy as it had been on the day of their wedding. She wanted him to lie down with her on the floor under the fish's jaws, to rub the fabric of her dresses and make them rustle pleasantly, and slip a hand up her thighs.

But out of the shell house stepped the snake woman, enveloped in a chador, followed by her long-armed flunkey. Her lips were colorless. She laid a hand on Shahin's back and simperingly rebuked him: "Who is this crazy girl? Why is she shouting that she's your wife? By your God, Shahin, *toré khoda,* who is she?"

Flora wanted Shahin to chop the strange woman's fair hair with her father's big butcher's knife, to uproot and pluck it out by the handful, to slit her neck and make all her pearls scatter. The wind from the sea rang in Flora's ears, scissors jangled in the air, their blades snapping rapidly, and Flora heard Manijoun's mutterings and Miriam Hanoum's shouts: "Flora! Leave the scissors alone! You're making little demons! Don't you know that's how the demons make children? The house will be full of little demons! Flora, enough, stop it now!"

"Enough, Flora! Stop it now!" When she opened her eyes the fish and Shahin were were both gaping at her, and her hands were tearing at the yellow hair of the snake woman, who was squealing in pain.

"Enough, Flora, *beleshkon,* leave her alone, I tell you, leave her alone...," Shahin yelled.

Flora was standing upright, legs apart, eyes glaring, a handful of yellow hair caught in her fingers. The bitter taste of the watermelon vomit rose in her throat and filled her mouth. She felt the wind drying the tears on her cheeks. Shahin was stroking his new wife's head with a comforting hand, while with the other he smoothed her silk gown. Flora saw how ugly his embarrassed face looked, how short he was, how deep the bays in his hair, how pale the ringworm scars on his balding pate. She turned around and pursued her own shadow toward the shore. She heard the snake woman screeching behind her: "Shahin, come back, you hear me? Shahin, come home at once!"

Flora kept tripping on her own feet, stumbling, rising and running on with bruised knees, trailing the horse blanket on the ground and raising a cloud of dust.

"Flora, wait." She heard Shahin behind her. "Wait, I tell you..." But she did not curb her clumsy galloping legs, her swinging arms, her bouncing chins.

"Mind the baby, Flora!"

She slowed down and dropped on the sand. Shahin fell to his knees beside her, took the horse blanket from her head and wrapped it around her body, stroked her flushed face, brushing it with his fingertips and pacifying her the way she loved, whispering, "My girl, you're my girl." He took off his shirt and bound her wounded knee with it, his sweat stinging the abrasions that blossomed redly through the cloth. Flora knew that the grasshopper on his tail was rasping and its colored wings were fluttering. Shahin whispered his lies into her ear, his hand shielding his soft, excited voice from the wind and the booming waves.

He had met the Baha'i woman Lily at her stall in the bazaar of Babol Sar, where she sold little cloth-stoppered jars of precious snake oil, a cure for rheumatism, weak bones, and inflamed joints. She told him that she herself made the preparation, and when he asked who the man was who crushed the heads of the poisonous reptiles for her, her glance turned and wandered over the pavement, and a smile spread on her colorless lips. Her slender, frail body aroused his suspicion and curiosity. When she finally told him her secret, that a family of snakes lived in the wall of her house, Shahin said good-bye to his loyal apprentice, tied his donkey in her courtyard, and promptly married her.

In his first few nights in the tall, two-storied house Shahin was afraid to fall asleep. Dreaming, he saw elongated silvery serpents rising from the cellars and stinging him to death with their forked tongues. The blue and green snakes that twined on the Baha'i woman's arms and hands also terrified him. When he shut his eyes, they glided down her long fingers and pierced him through her nails, coiling around his neck. Lying sleepless, Shahin listened all night long to the snakes slithering through the walls of the big house and under the marble floor, rubbing their scales against each other. The rustle of their scales sounded to him like a slow, absorbed leafing through the pages of a book, and he wondered who was sitting there reading.

Lily learned to hold him tight on stormy, thundery nights, and Shahin grew accustomed to sleeping with her snake arms around his neck. But he took care to walk about the house in high thick-soled shoes, and hid his thin slippers, which covered only the toes, in the back of a drawer.

Lily's mother, so she told him, had discovered the reptiles living in her house three years before her death. One night she happened to forget a wooden bowl full of sweetened milk down in the cellar. In the morning the milk was gone, and in its place was a gleaming pearl. The following night she left the bowl in the same corner, filled to the

brim with apple cider. In the morning there was a diamond in the bottom of the bowl.

On the third night the Baha'i woman's curiosity
hatched out of the egg of fear. She filled the bowl with
olive oil and hid in a corner, wrapped in a blanket. In the
early morning she saw through the mists of sleep six
gleaming snakes approaching the bowl and sipping the
offered oil. Before leaving, one of them took a gold coin
from the wall, dropped it into the bowl, and undulated
back to its hole.

Lily's mother did not reveal the secret to her husband.
She knew that men are foolish and impetuous and that her
husband would demolish the house to its foundations to
find the hidden treasure, and the snakes' vengeance would
persecute them to their dying day. When he asked why she
went down every night to the cellar, and who the milk and
ale, oil and wine were intended for, she replied vaguely,
"For the cats, the cats."

"Stupid old woman." He grinned and made a dismissive
gesture. "Takes good milk and gives it to cats."

By the time he died, she had in the cellar three big
earthen jars full of gold and precious gems, hidden under
a pile of worn goats' hair blankets.

Before she joined him in the grave, she revealed the
secret of the snakes to her only daughter Lily and made
her swear that she would never disclose it to a soul, not
even to her husband, even if she loved him dearly. Men, she
said, are greedy, impatient, and ungrateful. Only women,
who brood all their lives on the secrets of life and of the
kitchen, are capable of preserving the secrets of the cellar,
too, and of extracting blessings and remedies from the
snakes' venom. A year after making that vow, Lily entrusted

the secret to Shahin, who kissed her, smiling sweetly, and thought about his father and the silkworm breeding plant he had dreamed about.

One night, soon after they were married, Shahin told his Baha'i wife to bake him a sweetbread with raisins, because he was hungry. As she stood in the kitchen in the middle of the night, kneading the dough, with the oven fire casting long, slim shadows on her snowy face and fair hair, Shahin thought about throwing her into the flames, as his father had done to his mother, who was humming heartache songs to him. When the woman's white flesh began to sizzle, he thought and his eyes glittered, he would go down to the cellar with a hatchet, strike the six snakes and crush their heads, spattering the walls with their precious oil. Then he would smash the walls, too, dig down to the foundations and gather the sparkling treasure to his bosom. When Lily took the sweet loaf from the oven, Shahin tore its round cheeks and devoured it, absorbed in his glowing visions. Lily gazed at him in wonder, smiling a little smile and humming love songs, thinking that she had not known how much her little husband desired fresh bread. Absorbed in his imaginings, Shahin rose to look for a hatchet and was alarmed to discover that nothing was left of the bread but some crumbs, and of the fire—only ashes extinguished with sand. Lily wiped the cold perspiration from his face with her floured hands, graying his black bristles. His walleye watched her tossing her hair from shoulder to shoulder, extracting a last raisin from his mouth with her tongue, and asking if he was coming to bed to satisfy her hunger, too.

Shahin snuggled between her white breasts with his eyes shut and imagined that they were the mounds of treasure hidden in the fabric of her house. In his fantasies he heard the treasure calling to him in a shrill yearning voice: "Come to me, Shahin *azizam,* come to me, take me, take…" He sprawled on mounds of gold, diamonds, and gems, gathered them hungrily to his bosom, embraced them, and delicately pushed his fingers into the openings of oysters from which rosy pearls twinkled at him. When he woke, the snakes of Lily's arms were wound around his neck, their thin tongues pointing at his mouth, their lidless painted eyes staring, moaning with desire: "Aaaaa…"

Shahin leapt up: "The hatchet!" he cried in terror, extricating himself from her clasping thighs and holding his moist, erect member. "Where's my hatchet?"

He raised his fist to hit Lily on the head, but she wriggled and evaded the blow, and slid from the bed to the carpet. A satisfied smile lit her face, and a pale dawn lit the window overlooking the pistachio orchard.

* * *

"But Shahin, *azizam,* what about our baby? Did you forget our baby? Look at my belly, Shahin. I haven't swallowed a chicken."

"Of course I remember, Flora, of course I remember the baby, how could I forget? It was for you that I married the Baha'i, damn her, believe me, for you and for our baby…I always thought about you, *azizam,* about the honey and citron of your skin, and the cinnamon of your mouth…Even when I was with her, with that white ghost…But I was sure that you were always laughing, I didn't know you were crying…"

"And didn't you hear the song I sang to you on the roof, and didn't you cry when I peed on the chicken eggs,

Shahin? And didn't you wake up when I breathed the espand smoke into my soul, and yawned and yawned?"

"I heard, *azizam,* I heard everything." He kissed her on the forehead and led her back to the two-storied house, with its arched balconied windows that looked like doors. His chest was bare, and Flora laughed and hobbled behind him, limping like her sister, her big woman's breasts bouncing, her big child's eyes misting over, and a blush spread on her cheeks as if they had been chafed. He said to her that if she pretended to agree to be his second wife, they would go down to the cellar together, fill the plaid blanket with the treasure, and flee to Omerijan, to have the baby in the village and to stick their tongues out at the gentile urchins who had thrown plum stones at her. Flora tightened her grip on his hand and thought only about the nice coachman who would take them back to Julfah in his carriage, and how in return for his kindness she would give him back his horse blanket filled with pearls and diamonds and gold coins. When they were back among the pistachio trees and under the saw-toothed fish, Flora remembered the Baha'i's white baby.

"What will happen to her baby, when we go home and she stays here?" she asked, and at once regretted it and covered her mouth in dread.

"He'll be with his mother, don't you think about..." Shahin hushed her.

"Shahin, listen," she said in a loud whisper, "what do we need so much money for? Maybe we should just take the milk jugs, which are already full of lots of gold and diamonds..."

"Flora!" he barked at her, wide-eyed. "Remember what I told you." He lowered his voice and narrowed his eyes. "You have to do what I tell you, otherwise…" He shook his finger at her, and the Baha'i's flunkey appeared at the door.

Shahin led her under a tree, spread the blanket, and told her to lie down. Speaking softly, he again described the treasure hidden under the ground. The spring water babbled into his story, and Flora at last found the sleep she had searched for the previous night in the alleys of Omerijan. In her dream she was imprisoned with Mamou's baby in a pickle jar, and beyond the glass the world became immense and its people giants.

The two-storied house had originally been a single-storied one. Its walls were plastered with thick, rough clay and were not inlaid with seashells. The fish, too, was still swimming placidly in the sea. It was the house of Menashé Nahidyan, a prosperous Jewish merchant who could read the writing of the English, and who left it to his clever son Raphael. Since Raphael did not yet have a wife to fill the rooms with her sons, he let his younger brother, the stupid Mashíah, live there with him.

The brothers Nahidyan could not eat bread or cakes, beans, meat, or fowl. If they so much as tasted the forbidden foods, they were immediately covered with itchy red patches on their skin. By morning the rash would be gone, but only after a sleepless night in which they scratched themselves furiously, tormented by urticaria. Their mother heaped their plates with cheeses, fish, and fruit, and filled their hands with sweets. Throughout their childhood they had squares of French chocolate melting in their pockets, and their sweat was like sugar, yet they were both thin and feeble. They did not inherit their father's handsome, sturdy physique, their mustaches were mere fuzz, and the oily pimples never disappeared from their faces. But they did learn from their father how to trade with the English in sugar, almonds, and sunflower oil, and to buy gigantic rounds of halva from the Turks.

Yet their great wealth came to them by accident, not through the elder brother's cleverness, but thanks to the younger brother's stupidity.

"*Five thousand pounds sugar cubes, five thousand pounds granulated sugar, one thousand pounds bitter almonds, five thousand bottles sunflower oil*—and remember to write it in letters as big as spiders," Raphael kept repeating from the shelves.

"Should I say it again, my stupid idiot donkey brother? One more time?" he said everything three times, quite loud, emphasizing every word to make sure they entered Mashíah's ears, which stuck out on the sides of his head like big wings. Mashíah went to the Babol postal clerk and copied the order in the fine handwriting he was so proud of, his tongue sticking out of the corner of his mouth and his eyebrows knitted together into a long sweaty hedge. He drew the letters in india ink, linking their curly tails, decorating the punctuation marks, and worked so hard that he unwittingly added a splendid round zero to the quantity of loose sugar his brother had ordered.

The postal clerk smiled and nodded at the big foreign letters, laid the telegram on the letters scales, quoted a double price, and told Mashíah he was going to dispatch the letter on the back of a fast dromedary camel, which could cover the distance to Isfahan in ten days, unlike a double-humped Bactrian camel, which did it in twenty. The statement sounded reasonable to Mashíah's big ears and small wit.

Winter and spring passed, and the ears of the elder

brother Raphael caught the tinkling of camel bells approaching from the city gate, bearing on their backs his consignment of sugar, almonds, and oil. The tinkling was louder and merrier than ever, and when Raphael put his head out of the window he could not see the end of the golden camel caravan. He drew out his belt and whipped his stupid brother Mashíah until he feigned death. Then the two of them cleared out all the rooms in the house, piling the furniture and carpets by the stream under the pistachio trees. Towers of sugar boxes rose in every corner, completely devouring the stone pavement and darkening the windows. The rounds of halva, bottles of oil, and sacks of almonds were shoved into the cellar, and throughout the summer the brothers slept like mourners on a narrow mattress that they laid on the piece of carpet left exposed near the door. At night Raphael hit his brother, slapped him, and pinched him, and they both wept and pretended to die. They drank too-sweet tea, grew as fat as their father, and drove away the armies of big black ants by beating big tambour drums.

This was the year of the great drought. The wells and fishponds dried up, the fields, melon patches, and plantations withered, cellars and barns emptied. But the light burned in the darkened rooms of the brothers Nahidyan. They were besieged not only by the inhabitants of Babol Sar, but by villagers from all around, who heard the rumor about the sugar mine. The boxes were emptied of the white grains and filled with silver, and when people's money ran out, the boxes were filled with gold jewelry, diamond rings, and pearl necklaces, pots of opium and bowls of hashish, ornamental copper vessels and bolts of silk.

Mashíah and Raphael added another story to their house, with arched windows fronted with little balconies, laid fine marble on the floors of both levels, covered the outer walls with seashells, and hung the gaping fish above the front door. When Shah Mohammed came to the throne and riots broke out all over the kingdom, the brothers went down to the cellar and buried their treasure in a pit they had dug under the paving. On their way to the city of Yazd both brothers, the clever one and the fool, were murdered, but all that the bandits found in their belongings were a few pistachio-nut shells, some almonds, and crumbling sugar cubes. A Baha'i family without sons settled in the two stories of the abandoned house, and a family of snakes moved into the basement.

* * *

"But I'm not tired now, I slept outside," said Flora, and the moths that entered the house with her danced above her head.

Lily summoned the long-armed flunkey and told him to lay a mattress for Flora on the ground floor, then ordered Flora, as if she were a sulky child, to follow the servant to her bed. Flora forgot the promise she had given Shahin when he was binding her wounded knees, and dug in her heels.

"Flora, go to sleep," said Shahin with a warning look, but she stared over her rounded belly at her toes, which stuck out of the tips of her worn felt shoes.

"Are you listening to me, Flora?" He came close and took hold of her chin, raising her face to remind her with a look of what she had promised. But Flora shook her heavy head, and her disheveled hair moved from side to side with her breasts.

"I want to sleep with you."

"Flora, sweetie," Shahin hissed, pressing his fingernails into her shoulder until she winced with pain, "go to sleep now."

"With you." She swung her knees rhythmically and shrugged her aching shoulders like a spoiled, unruly child.

Shahin and his two wives walked up the stairs with the little oil lamps to Lily's room, which was full of shadowy recesses. In the dimness Flora noticed that the floor was not covered with carpets laid one upon the other, but with simple hides of cattle and the cured skins of wild beasts. Their odors overcame the salty aroma of the sea that permeated the walls, and they felt good to her bare feet. Her tiredness was gone, and she wanted to explore the room, but Lily abruptly blew out the candle and complete darkness fell.

"Shahin?" Flora called out in the dark, hearing the moths fluttering about her ears. "Shahin, where are you? I can't see you."

"I'm here," he replied hoarsely after a moment. Flora walked toward his voice like a blind woman, her hands outstretched, until she reached him and wrapped her arms around his neck. She wanted to lay her head on his breast and stroke his thinning hair, but he seemed to have grown nice soft hair, and her astonished hands encountered a pair of breasts. She touched them curiously and suddenly felt Lily's hard little belly pushing against her.

"Ha ha ha, stupid girl…" Lily laughed gratingly. Flora recoiled, rocked slightly and fell face down on odorous camel skins.

"Come on, Flora." Shahin gave her his hand, raised her, and pulled her to his wife's bed. "You must go to sleep."

Flora felt his hand, found the manly hairs on the joints, and squeezed it between her fat fingers.

"It's me," said Shahin. "Easy now, Flora, easy." She took two cautious steps after him. Reaching one of the recesses, he supported her back and laid her down gently, careful not to touch her wounds. Flora felt his breath on her neck. Her body was longer than the mattress, and she drew up her feet. Shahin covered her with a quilt and lay down alongside, turning his curved back to her. Even without touching it, Flora knew that his backbone bulged through his shirt, and her mind's eye saw his cherished face and his weak eye twitching persistently.

She wanted to give him a fold of her dress to rub, but she heard Lily's silk gown rustling on the bed. She heard the Baha'i woman tucking the quilt around herself, uttering a weary little sigh, and snuggling up to Shahin. A green snake reached out to his loins and a blue one to his face. Flora clung to her husband's back, one hand on his hair, the other on his buttocks, and yawned sweetly. Silence fell in the room. Through the susurration of the wind and her gathering dreams, Flora felt Lily's long nails moving on Shahin's body and flickering over hers, too. Shahin's hair stood on end, pricking her palm, and her skin tingled. Shahin groaned, trying to stifle the sounds breaking from his throat, and moved between his wives like a dancer between tongues of flame. Thousands of pores burst open in Flora's skin and gaped like deep pits. She heard their two hearts beating together wildly and the heavy pounding of her heart by itself. She heard the rustle of clothes being taken off and buttons undone, and in the darkness Lily's white body gleamed momentarily and vanished under the shadow of her husband's body.

"Shhh…," Shahin whispered in his wife's ear, rebuking her eagerness. His eye squinted uneasily at Flora, while

Lily's eyes rolled up to the ceiling. Flora closed her eyes, and a cold sweat broke out of all the pits in her body, reviving the smell of watermelon vomit from the previous night. When she opened them, Shahin was piercing Lily's body, burrowing into it, and the two of them squirmed. The tattooed snakes writhed over their heads.

"It's not nice, what you're doing, Shahin. I'm going home."

Flora slid from the mattress to the skins and furs spread on the floor, pushed herself upright, and sought to leave the room, which was full of recesses, snakes, and shadows. She picked up her shoes, tucked them under her arm, and began to move slowly, one hand feeling the wall for an opening, the other covering her ear, to block the others' rhythmic moans. When she found an iron bar thrust through a wall ring she tugged it out, quickly opened the door, and put out one foot and then another to the stairs, but the sea wind gathered her to itself.

Instead of the door to the passage, Flora's groping hands had opened a balcony window. She stumbled on the sill and glided on the wind over the low parapet, and her shoes flew with her. Shahin's donkey looked up and smiled at her when she landed beside it among the trees, while windfall pistachio fruits dropped on her hair and moths circled over her head.

CHAPTER NINETEEN

WHEN NAZIE COME OUT OF the mosque, the palm trees in the avenue sheltered her and caressed her head with their fronds. The slender fingers of the wintry midday sun passed through and toyed with her hair. Her head burned between her shoulders, still draped in the strange chador. At first she tried to stop the bleeding with her hands, but the blood ran between her fingers and down her neck, collecting over and under the chador. She dropped her hands and let it flow from her split earlobes as from open taps. Her face twitched with pain, and her heart galloped. Men from the mosque courtyard stared at her back and the market people at her face.

The peasants on their mules, the peddlers who trundled their handcarts between the bazaar stalls, and the housewives in their homes, alley cats, dogs, children—they all stopped and stared at her. The beggars' empty mouths hung open. The hawkers stopped singing, and their customers turned around to look at the painted face of Nazichi Ratoryan, the Jewish orphan, at her muddied dress and the camel-hair chador that was slowly turning red.

"One minute she's a Zafarollah pigeon, the next minute

she's a Delkasht peacock," she heard someone exclaiming as she walked past, setting one foot in front of the other along a straight line she drew amid the mucky puddles on the road to the Jubareh, her eyes as always searching for dropped coins that might wink at her from the filthy pavement. But her heart was leaping from her rib cage.

When she left the mosque, she tipped her head forward, nodding quickly in gratitude like a pecking pigeon. But the gold earrings no longer tinkled in her ears, and the fishes no longer swung the tiny coins on the ends of their tails. They were swimming in a little pool in the *mullah's* open palm and diving into its old furrows. Even before she sliced her ears, she had felt a wave of pain rising from inside her. Despair spun crisscross threads before her eyes, hiding *mullah* Ja'afar's face. But when she tore the gold from her flesh, the threads broke and everything became clear. The pain was so rousing, and the gushing blood so astounding, that Nazie wanted more. When she saw it dripping on the hunted deer carpet, she looked straight into the *mullah's* goggling eyes and demanded that he grant her request.

At first she did not know where to go. Should she mingle with the crowd in the bazaar and bring the news to Moussa first—the shop was so near, its entrance as usual clustered with idlers and peddlers selling sweets or salt-and-pepper shakers, Moussa's apron as bloody as her dress, the butcher's knife in his hand throwing glints on his pimply face—and he is not thinking about Shahnaz Tamizi but only about her, her alone, and he's waiting for her to come as she had promised, and he would wrap a chicken for her, tie it with a string, and tell her what he wanted for supper...Or should she run home first, shake the late-rising Miriam Hanoum, confront her morning yawns, and say: "*Ameh bozorg, ameh bozorg,* I can marry Moussa, the *mullah* said I can marry Moussa today."

Nazie gathered up her skirts and ran home, to pull the blankets off her aunt's face and give her the glad news about the wedding, as if she were her mother, because she was very anxious to please her. Emerging from the marketplace, she passed through the moon gate and did not go past the synagogue straight to the Jubareh, but circled the village wall, to avoid the villagers' mean eyes and inquisitive questions. Yet even so, when she passed the noisy flour mill of the Jewish miller Suleiman, the son-in-law of the late Pinhas, the laborers stopped carrying the sacks of grain and followed her with their eyes.

When she reached the turning in the alley, she saw Miriam Hanoum standing in the house gate, her head in the black chador turning this way and that, her eyes restless. Homa sat amid the puddles on the lower step at her mother's feet, resting her hump against a gatepost, her legs apart, the crooked one turning to the house, the straight one sticking out into the street. Homa was waving her arms wildly as she always did when she talked, and Nazie could hear her shouts from as far as the Jews' gate, but could not make out the words. She wanted to run to her aunt and cry in her lap, but when she came near, she saw that Miriam Hanoum's face was tense and she was spitting curses through clenched teeth.

"Where's Flora? Have you seen Flora?" her aunt barked as soon as she saw her. Homa raised herself awkwardly, her eyes staring, and Nazie remembered the cool bedding on her cousin's empty bed.

"*Vavaila!* What's happened to you? You think you've turned into a lady overnight?" Homa caught the hem of

Flora's wedding dress and flapped it, and Nazie stumbled and fell. Homa's fingers pierced the air. "And where's my idiot sister who let you put on this dress to go to the market?"

"God punish you, Nazie, how did you get all this blood on you?" Miriam Hanoum shrieked, then bit her tongue. "Where've you been that this happened to you?"

"And where's my sister Flora gone in the middle of the night, huh? You must know where she went." Homa pulled Nazie's arm as though to tear it off. Nazie shook her head and stood up.

"Look at her. Don't you lie to us, Nazie. Crazy Manijoun saw her going out in her dream. Where did she go, the idiot—maybe she wanted another watermelon?"

"She's not at Nosrat's, and Sultana said she hasn't been to her house, and Fathaneh, damn her eyes, isn't home, and Hayim the beggar hasn't seen her—but they all tell stories as dirty as their faces. Homa and I have turned the alley inside out, and no Flora. Nazie, by your life, where has she gone?"

"May I drop dead if I know. In the morning I didn't see her in her bed..." In her agitation Nazie took the chador off her head, uncovering her bleeding, split earlobes. Miriam Hanoum struck herself on the breasts and slapped the back of her hand.

"God help you, Nazie, what did you do to yourself? By your mother's grave, tell me where you threw the earrings I gave you!"

"I don't have them anymore, *ameh bozorg*." Nazie bit her lower lip. "Forgive me, God in heaven saw that I didn't have a choice, I had to give them to the *mullah* in the bazaar mosque..."

"Waï, waï, waï!" Miriam Hanoum broke in, scratching her lovely face. "And he, damn him for all time—and you, too, wretched child, throwing our honor to the dogs—was it he made you all bloody like this—may his gentile eyes drop out of his head and burn this morning in this sun…?"

"Yes."

"Oh, Nazie, God take you if you're lying to me…" Miriam Hanoum's eyes narrowed suspiciously, and Homa's eyes flared with fury.

"I swear, my life for yours if I'm lying," Nazie squeaked excitedly. "And he said that for the earrings I gave him I can marry Moussa tonight, and that Moussa and me should come to him to the *hammam* at midday, and he'll give us a paper, and tonight we'll give it to *mullah* Netanel to make Moussa a groom and me a bride, and he said we must do everything simply and quietly, so nobody will give us away to the officials, or we'd be done for, so he said, *ameh bozorg,* so help me." Nazie's eyes filled with tears as big as stones.

"Azizam!" cried Miriam Hanoum. "Congratulations, *azizam!"*

She pressed Nazie's head to her fragrant bosom and lavished kisses on the dripping and drying blood, on Nazie's painted face, and on the strange chador. Even Homa stopped pinching Nazie's arm and hugged her lovingly.

"Nazie, *azizam,* swear to me by this sun, by this sky—he said today? Today, he said?"

Nazie nodded, her head caught between the four big breasts. They moaned and stifled the joyous ululation that rose in their throats. She did not want to pull her head out of the suffocating warm nest in which she snuggled, but she did wish that her mother would push in between Homa and Miriam Hanoum and embrace her, and for Flora's wild laughter to break into their midst and for her snorts to accompany the shaking of the four breasts against her body. The kerchief slipped from her head, and with it her tears began to fall, blossoming like sweat flowers on the women's chadors, which were warm from their bodies.

"No, Nazie, don't cry on your wedding day," Homa scolded her, drying her face and smearing the traces of paint. "It's a day of celebration, not of mourning—nobody's dead, God forbid, right?"

"Come." Miriam Hanoum cupped Nazie's little face to stop her tears, and wiped her little nose. "The sun's almost in the middle of the sky and we have preparations to make. We'll fill the pots with water and put them in the sun to warm for the bath of our little bride."

Nazie and Homa were drawing buckets from the cistern, where the surface ice had melted since morning and the water had cleared, when Nazie suddenly thought about Moussa in the market, cutting up fowls, flies buzzing around his head, unaware that his wedding day had arrived. Homa was sent to tell him and his father to shut up shop and come home.

"Tell him," Miriam Hanoum shouted after her, "to load the mule of Parviz, the little porter, with everything we need from the market—he should buy a lot of *labash* and Barbary bread, and we'll need dried lemons, won't we, Nazie?"

"Yes, and fish, too, and eggs."

"Yes, fish and eggs for the blessings, and tell Janjan Furush to set aside some coriander and tarragon for me, because we're having a big feast—but she must keep her big mouth shut—tell her, that big idiot—or better still don't tell her anything. They made my daughter into a whore in their fantasies. But where is Flora? Where is that girl, damn her, as if the watermelon swallowed her up—so much trouble she's brought this house...Don't tell Janjan anything, you hear?"

* * *

Miriam Hanoum captured the transparent sun that shone palely in the sky in a big saucepan full of cold water. She gazed deeply into it and raised it up to the sky, doubting the heat of the sun. Finally she set down a couple of stones, placed a small grate on them, and built a fire under the pot. The water heated slowly, and vapor began to rise from it.

Nazie had not seen Miriam Hanoum so happy and lively since the day she took her in. When Flora comes home, she won't believe what Nazie will tell her. A new spirit, like a demon's energy, seized Miriam Hanoum, who ran around the house, the braided crown loose on her shoulders and big smiles joining her lips and eyes. Her fine hands came to life and snapped in the air like busy scissors. She opened all the house windows, made a bundle of all the sour bedsheets and tied its corners into a sack. She carried the bags of feathers, which were strewn about the house, into the girls' room, together with the small kitchen table and its chairs. Manijoun, too, was dragged into that room, curled up in her basket, and her old woman's eyes almost popped out of her head.

"*Vavaila!* What, what's happened, is anyone dead?" she screeched.

"We have a wedding today," Miriam Hanoum trilled.

"We have a bridegroom and bride today!" And she kissed her mother-in-law on her wrinkled forehead between the raised eyebrows.

"A wedding…What wedding? Are you going to marry me off? Who's my bridegroom? Let me out of here, I need a beautiful dress, I need flowers in my hair, oh God, what kind of groom did you get me?"

"A tall man, strong as a dog, as a wolf, as a horse, Manijoun…" Miriam Hanoum laughed and left the girls' room. On the carpets in the main room she spread large tablecloths, which still showed faint islands of grease and wine stains from Flora's wedding. Around the *sofreh* she arranged embroidered down-filled cushions, and the mattresses were rolled up against the walls. Then she went to the bean shed and dragged out a bag of flour, a bag of rice, packets of sugar and salt, beans and lentils, a jar of wine and many pots of honey.

"Oh Flora…What I'm going to do to that girl when she comes home—I'll break her arms and legs, see if I don't—running around in the middle of the night…" The odor of the melting *dombeh* spread through the house like the smell of fire.

"Come here now, Nazie, come over here, *azizam,*" Miriam Hanoum called her from inside the bean shed. "All this is yours," Nazie heard her saying. "Your mother gave me these things for you, to give you on the day of your wedding with Moussa."

Nazie stood in the doorway as Miriam Hanoum raised the creaking lid of a large wooden chest in the corner, its cracks and locks thick with dust. Nazie, who had always assumed that it was one of Flora's dowry chests, discovered that it was filled to the brim with things that had belonged to her mother. There was a mirror with its casing, an embroidered coat, and a short one, three dresses and a negligée, a comb with some of her mother's hairs caught between its teeth, three Bokhara rugs, a spouted jug with a copper bowl, silver candlesticks and pewter bowls, and a perfume spray filled with a red fluid whose strong scent spread through the shed. Then Miriam Hanoum opened a purple velvet bag and took out a turquoise jewel set in a tarnished silver chain and a gold ring embossed with pomegranates.

"Before she died," Miriam Hanoum said, "your mother owed me ten eggs which she borrowed but never returned. If she hadn't taken them, I'd have had ten fat chickens, and by this time they'd have produced many eggs and chicks and a lot of money. So, Nazie *azizam,* I'll take this necklace now and we'll forget about your mother's debt to me…Well, come on, what are you looking at? Take everything and let's go, half the day is almost over."

Miriam Hanoum carried the boiling pot from the yard into the house and set it down in the girls' room, which looked like an untidy storeroom. Manijoun was sitting in her corner, all excited, her feet tucked under her, her black fingers undoing her braids and loosening the yellow-white corn husk hair. Giggling like an excited bride, she licked her palms and wiped the saliva on her hair. "I'll build a bath, la la laï…," she sang as she washed.

"I'll build a bath, la la laï, with forty columns and forty windows, la la laï…," sang Miriam Hanoum as she peeled off Nazie's chador. She pulled the butterfly knots in Flora's wedding gown, and the dress fell below Nazie's childish nipples, which stared like a pair of bold eyes.

Miriam Hanoum caught the folds of the dress and lifted it up in the air. Left in her worn cotton underpants, Nazie hugged herself. The chill made the tiny hairs on her body stand on end. Miriam Hanoum's cold fingers pulled her underpants down, and Nazie leaned on her aunt's shoulders to step out of them. She felt her bones boring into Miriam Hanoum's flesh and her goose pimples pricking it like thousands of tiny needles.

"How small you are, *azizam,* how small." Miriam Hanoum clapped her hands, her eyes examining Nazie all over, as if seeing her for the first time. "We should feed you peanuts and almonds to fatten you up…Come on then, get in, half the day is gone…" Nazie stepped into the heavy iron tub and curled up in it like Manijoun in her basket. Miriam Hanoum poured the hot water from the pot into the tub.

"Hot! *Ameh bozorg,* it's hot!"

"Forty columns and forty windows, la la laï, la la laï…" The scalding water reached Nazie's neck, and turned rosy from the blood.

"I'll fill the bath with rose water, to bathe my bride in. La la laï, la la laï, my bride's hair flows like water, her face glows like the moon…" Miriam Hanoum's hair flowed in waves over her shoulders, and her face grew round and shiny as she sang. She scrubbed Nazie with soap and a scratchy herb sponge until the girl's skin turned crimson. Her fingernails scraped her scalp and worked up a lather in her hair. Soap bubbles burst in Nazie's ears and drops of water ran like tears from her burning earlobes. Nazie gritted her teeth.

Coated in honey as in a thick blanket, she felt the pain fading slowly. Miriam Hanoum scooped handfuls of honey from the jars and spread it on her skin until her bones stopped trembling. The coating of honey was cooked by the body's heat like salt on the fire and softened the tiny hairs which stuck out of the open pores. Smeared with sweetness to her eyebrows, Nazie was intoxicated by the warm scent, and her rounded face shone like a golden Shiraz orange. Miriam Hanoum did not overlook a single part of her body, and she glistened all over. The sticky fingers flitted on Nazie's armpits and nape, like a belly dancer at a betrothal party. The pores of her skin opened like thousands of little mouths and greedily sipped the honey.

"You want a little gold, too, Manijoun, our bride?" Miriam Hanoum, her eyes glittering, teased her mother-in-law, and smeared a little honey on her mustache. Manijoun, her hair damp and flattened with saliva, stuck out her tongue and licked her upper lip. Nazie sucked a pointed knee, and the honey ran thick and sweet into her throat. Festive twinkles of light danced in through the window.

The sounds and smells from behind the bead curtain told Nazie that Miriam Hanoum was chopping onions and throwing them into the seething mutton fat, to glaze and turn golden. She thought about her mother's jewelry, hidden from her among the sacks of lentils and grain, and felt angry about the years she had lived without a comb, a mirror, or scent, envying Flora her jewelry.

✳ ✳ ✳

A donkey bell rang in the alley and stopped. Crates were dragged along the paving stones, and sacks were flung down on the ground. The low front door creaked on its iron hinges, and the voice of Miriam Hanoum's husband, bringing home the rumors that were flying in the village, mixed with that of Homa searching for Flora and Miriam Hanoum's raging curses. Parviz the little porter took advantage of the tumult to demand excessive payment, and Homa's husband haggled with him. In between curses, Miriam Hanoum welcomed her son joyously and fell on his neck with kisses. But to Nazie's torn ears Moussa's excited voice overcame all the others.

"Where's Nazie?" she heard him shouting. She wanted to shake off the heavy coat of honey and run to him. She stood up, but a sudden wind blew in from the alley, shaking the windows and slamming them against the walls, and before Nazie's wide-open eyes overturned the bags of feathers that had been heaped beside Manijoun's basket. Goose down chased chicken feathers, filled the air, spinning like snowflakes, followed by dust and leaves. Nazie tried to escape, but the windblown stuff stuck to the honey on her naked body. She saw herself looking like a partly plucked fowl and wept sweet tears. Her lips stuck together and could not be parted, her sweat mingled with the honey, fluffy down filled her ears, and her whole body itched as if it had grown a fur coat. Manijoun shrieked at the sight of the demon child who had blown in from the alley, and Miriam Hanoum burst in like the wind.

"Vavaila!" she bawled. "What have you done to yourself? Get up, get up—again you're crying? Didn't I tell you you mustn't cry today? It brings bad luck—because of your tears the demons turned you into a chicken. I told you, didn't I? Get up, what's the matter with you, you want to drive me crazy? Isn't it enough that Flora has disappeared now of all times? Who knows where that girl is and what she's doing with herself."

"Ma," they heard Moussa's tense voice, "what's happened to Nazie?"

"It's all right, she's coming right out," Miriam Hanoum replied hastily, shutting the door and bolting the window. "Get up, wash yourself again. Moussa's here and is waiting for you outside. How long can a groom wait for his bride?"

The water was tepid. Nazie floated on it, the honey on her lips as tasteless as wax. Her aunt plucked the pointy feathers off her, scratched her skin with her fingernails, exposing the gluey, darkening honey. Nazie bit her own shoulders and with her teeth pulled off some stubborn feathers.

"Nazie?" she heard Moussa calling her through the door. "Nazie?" His dog howled in the alley like a wolf pack, and Manijoun sobbed with fright.

She had to make haste, Moussa could not contain himself, he could wait for her no longer.

Miriam Hanoum expressed all her rage against Flora and the rumors her husband brought from the market, all her grief and anxieties, in brushing Nazie's hair. She raked the hair with the comb and plowed the scalp with her fingers. "Don't move, *azizam,* sit quietly and let me comb you," she said through gritted teeth. Nazie held her breath and stifled her moans. Her forehead creased with pain, then stretched with the rest of her body to the roots of her hair. Odors of cooking spread through the bead curtain and entered the room through the cracks around the door.

"What stinking stories people invent out of their dirty heads, they should be covered with dust." The teeth of the comb, with the hairs from her dead mother's head, pricked Nazie's scalp like the tines of a fork.

"I swear to you by this midday sun—Shahin should die a gentile's death, and leave me my girl in the house, with her watermelon belly and all. That would be better—a widow, not a slut that follows her hot hole all over the village at night."

Mahasti's hairs and Nazie's were knotted up into a tangled dusty ball.

"It's because of him, just because of him, that we got all these troubles on our house. He took a lucky child and made her into a crazy woman—all on account of the moon eclipse. There," said Miriam Hanoum, extracting a soft little goose feather from Nazie's hair. "One feather was left in your head." She waved it before Nazie's eyes and tapped it with a fingertip to make it drop.

"Wait, I need it." She changed her mind and caught the feather as it floated slowly down to the floor. Her fist swallowed it, and she bent down to catch more feathers, but they were insufficient, and she took a few scoops from the bags. Peering through the curtain of her hair, Nazie saw Miriam Hanoum stuffing feathers into a pair of socks from Flora's cradle. She opened a gap in the curtain and watched her aunt tearing a white bedsheet into broad strips.

"Up, up, *azizam,* Moussa is waiting for his bride." Miriam Hanoum raised her from the carpet. She pressed the feather balls to Nazie's flat chest, one on each nipple. Nazie's hair hung down over the feather breasts.

"Now we'll tie them," said Miriam Hanoum and wound the bedsheet strips around Nazie's chest and shoulderblades.

"*Mashallah, Baha, Baha,* see how you've grown, *azizam,* how you've grown!" Her aunt hugged her, her great breasts pressing the featherballs to Nazie's beating heart.

When at last Nazie emerged, washed and barefooted, from the girls' room, fish were sizzling in oil in Miriam Hanoum's iron skillet, Homa was stitching pullets stuffed with rice, raisins, and chipped carrots, Homa's husband was rinsing the *sabzi* in water, and Miriam Hanoum's husband stood in the doorway, asking the passersby if they had seen Flora. Many peddlers arrived in the alley, following the bell of little Parviz's donkey, which was laden with all kinds of good things.

"Spinach, marrows! Spinach, marrows!" shouted a man pushing a loaded barrow and swinging a pair of scales. After him came the shepherd, his arrival announced by the bleating of his flock. "Your daughter Flora?" he shouted. "No, I haven't seen her. Maybe she drank too many cups of spit from the neighbors and got drunk, poor thing." The other peddlers around the house guffawed with him.

"Shut the door!" Miriam Hanoum shouted to her husband. "I don't want them coming into the house with their eyes. Homa, damn you, what did you say to Janjan Furush that brought this crowd outside?"

"Nothing, on my life!"

"Miriam Hanoum, beet red as blood, tomato sweet as honey!" came the cries from the alley.

"So how come all the sweets and pistachio sellers are turning up here, you idiot? You told her we're having a wedding?"

"No, ma, no! She asked me, burst her eyes, she asked how come I need so much *sabzi*—I hope all her *sabzi* sticks in her throat...I didn't know what to tell her...Ma, I only said that Shahin and his donkey were back in the village, and she said, so where is Flora, and I said she's gone to do the henna and to bathe for him in the *hammam,* and she said, so how come your father's looking for her all over the village? She also said that people say they saw her last night walking..."

"Shut up, Homa, shut up, or I'll stuff your mouth with eggs, you should choke from talking so much!" Moussa broke into his sister's speech, and her embarrassed husband gazed into the water pot.

When Nazie came into the kitchen, she saw that Moussa was still dressed in his butcher's clothes, and was shelling boiled eggs with his black fingers. He cracked each one on his bent knee and crushed the shells.

"There's the lady bride, at last—washed yourself till it turned nighttime," grumbled Miriam Hanoum. Everyone looked at Nazie and at Moussa, who approached her, tall and smiling, shedding bits of eggshell.

"The wind came in...," she apologized with a flushed face, and his heart went out to her. He saw the split earlobes, the soft feather breasts, the tears glistening in her eyes.

"Look, I bought you new shoes," he murmured quickly, so that her tears would not fall on the eggshells. "Bride's shoes." High above her head he held a white box, tied with string. Nazie looked up at the box sliding between his arms, and in her mind's eye she saw the pair of laquered white high-heeled shoes that had called to her from Shimshon Shaharudi's stall in the bazaar, and that she dreamed of wearing at her wedding. Moussa knelt at her feet on the Kashani carpet and put down the closed box.

"I measured them by my hand," he said, laying his open palm on the carpet. He took her ankle as carefully as if she were a fledgling, and gently placed her bare foot on his palm.

"You see, Nazie, exactly! Your foot is exactly the size of my hand," he whispered, and Homa sighed with relief.

"I told him to leave the shoes, because there's no time," she said to Miriam Hanoum, jabbing at the air with the poultry needle. "And she'd have to try them on."

"She could've taken Flora's shoes, like she took her dress—God punish her for disappearing like this," Miriam Hanoum added, her eyes hidden by the smoke that rose from the fish skillet, her ears pricked to the sounds outside.

"I told him, but he wouldn't listen to me and didn't let me go until he found shoes for her. He turned the stall of Azet Shaharudi's husband upside down, searched and searched, and I swear, he's got the exact size of her foot."

"Could have taken a bigger size, to last a few years," Miriam Hanoum said sourly. "What, he imagines she'll always be a little girl?—She'll grow up in his hands."

"He didn't listen to me, but see how she's laughing now," Homa cooed.

Moussa untied the string and with a proud gesture took out of the box a pair of white, high-heeled shoes with silver buckles, but because they were plain unlaquered leather, Nazie thought they looked ordinary and unattractive. She searched for her mother among the women in the room, for a lap in which to hide her disappointed face. Moussa took her feet and slipped them one by one into the shoes, which fitted her perfectly. He did not notice that the tears in her eyes were not tears of joy.

"Aï, aï, they are small on me, Moussa, take them off, they're hurting me," said Nazie, and burst into bitter tears like a spoiled child.

"No, Nazie, don't cry," Moussa groaned in surprise.

"Don't cry, there, I've taken them off, and we'll change them at Shaharudi for a bigger pair, please don't cry…"

"*Vavaila,* again she's crying—and what for?" screamed Miriam Hanoum, choking from the smoke. "Today's her wedding day and she's bathing in her tears like a newborn baby! What's the matter, aren't you ashamed—you've got shoes, you've got breasts, and you've got a nice dowry—so what more do you want, *Khodaia,* what more?"

Everyone stared at Nazie with suspicion, at the girl who had torn her ears that morning in the mosque, had fluttered all over the village, and already her feet were bigger than Moussa's hands.

CHAPTER TWENTY

Wʜᴇɴ ᴛʜᴇ ꜰɪʀꜱᴛ ꜱᴛᴀʀ appeared in the sky of Omerijan, Nazie wanted to go to sleep. She rubbed her eyes with her fists, and her head drooped on her shoulder. The day's events flickered under her closed lids.

She lay down on the rug, letting her head sink into the ball of bedsheets bundled up by Miriam Hanoum, pressing her feather breasts together against her beating heart. She had tied a white kerchief on her head so that the guests would not see her torn earlobes. The rain pattered in the almond tree alley, but indoors the rooms whispered: "Flora...Flora...Flora..."

Nazie thought about the neighborhood children who, when darkness fell, spread their mattresses on the soft bedding of rugs. At this time brothers and sisters were hugging each other, falling asleep snugly like yolks in egg whites. When she and Flora, Moussa and Homa were small children, they, too, used to push their mattresses together at bedtime and rollick boisterously, jumping on the sprawling white bed, laughing and shouting, throwing pillows and tickling each other under the covers, until Miriam Hanoum swore and screamed at them to go to sleep, and then they would press buttocks to bellies, tuck heads into napes, and giggle softly until sweet slumber covered them all.

But once Moussa became a man, he was not allowed to sleep like a baby swaddled in girls' bodies, and had to curl up in the main room. Homa got married, and Flora— where was Flora now?

"A little bride we have today, *kuchik madar* she will be tomorrow…" Manijoun hummed the bridal song. She had trimmed her nails with her teeth and collected the yellow crescents neatly on the rug. She filed the trimmed nails by sucking them between her lips, then took them out one by one, spread her palms and gazed proudly at the manicure. She had rubbed the greasy sauce of the lunch rice on her face, making it shine turmeric-yellow like the plate.

Nazie's hair was drawn tight, with a solemn parting running down her head. She was wearing a white velvet dress from Mahasti's dowry chest, with a moth-eaten embroidered hem. Its skirts trailed on the floor, but below them gleamed the laquered shoes that Moussa had run and brought from Shaharudi's stall to replace the pair with the silver buckles. They were too big, but Nazie kept lifting her riddled skirts at every step to relish their beauty.

"Nazie, Nazie, *azizam,* where are you?" Miriam Hanoum shouted as she opened the door to the girls' room. "What, you've gone to sleep?…Went to bed, the lady bride. Was almost asleep already," she announced over her shoulder to the sitting room.

Trembling all over, Nazie extricated herself from the soft bundle of bedding. Suddenly she became aware of the murmuring of the guests in the house, as if she had woken up from a deep sleep.

"You can laugh," Manijoun said to her, her hair damp and her face bright yellow. "Go ahead and laugh at your grandmother, wait till you choke on the egg your bastard husband planted in your belly, stupid Flora."

Nazie thrust out the false breasts on her chest and left the room, the big laquered shoes slipping off her heels and clattering on the floor with every step, their drumming echoing her heart.

The women greeted her with subdued *gilli-li-li* cries, taking care not to let the neighbors hear wedding ululation coming from the house. Their kisses pricked her cheeks like skewers, and she felt that her face, without the colorful wedding makeup, was gray and ugly. The men with their trousers hitched high above their stomachs, the points of their mustaches curling downward, stood around Moussa, who was already waiting for her under the wedding canopy, as if in a hurry to go on to another wedding. Very softly, Mahatab Hanoum's flute trilled jolly wedding songs, while rabbi *mullah* Netanel the widower blessed the couple, wedging his big paunch between them.

"Tonight we have a little bride, tomorrow we'll have a *kuchik madar...*" The joyous songs were sung softly, as if they were doleful, wistful songs, and the expression on the guests' faces was intent, as if they could hear the whisper in Nazie's ears: "Flora...Flora...Flora..."

Only Manijoun's voice rose loud and clear from the closed girls' room. Nazie imagined her grandmother capering in her wicker basket like a bride at her wedding, her face gleaming in the dark with oil and tears.

"*Khodaia*, God, this lunatic, she'll ruin everything!" Miriam Hanoum hissed furiously to Sabiya Mansour, Manijoun's sister, as though it was all her fault, and disappeared behind the door. When she returned from the girls' room, her arms were folded like a bulwark on her bosom, Manijoun's voice was heard no more, and the rain fell harder.

Suddenly Nazie felt very tall under the canopy, her head almost touching it. She raised the velvet skirts that hid her shoes to see if she was floating, or if she had really grown that day unawares. But her feet were planted on the Kashani rug, swimming in the laquered shoes she had longed for.

"Congratulations, *mobaraket bashi,*" Miriam Hanoum muttered over her, kissing the air, her eyes turning restlessly to the windows. "Go outside now and bring the chickens from the *comejdoun* like a good bride, go on! The guests are hungry, me and Homa are going to bring in the fish and rice and everything from the kitchen. Go, *azizam,* go." Miriam Hanoum opened the door and pushed Nazie into the backyard.

Homa had earlier buried the pot with the stuffed chickens in the *comejdoun* under the citron tree. She had laid red-hot coals on the bottom of the big, oven-shaped hollow, placed the pot on top of them, and covered it with sacks and sand, to keep hot until the meal. Moussa's dog followed Nazie as she groped in the dark to reach the citron tree, holding up her skirts, her new shoes sinking in the mud and the thin veil on her head melting in the rain. She crouched beside the buried treasure and poked through the damp soil. But the pot was not there, only the scorched sacks in which it had been wrapped, and ashes that blackened her hands. Inside the brightly lit house the few guests were waiting for her, sprawled comfortably on the cushions around the *sofreh,* which was covered with steaming bowls full of rice, fish, herbs, and hard-boiled eggs. The glasses were red with wine, but the copper plates were empty, waiting for Nazie to come back with the chickens.

"*Ameh bozorg,* I can't find the food in the *comejdoun,*" she said on the doorstep, and the clapper hanging from the mouth of the lion doorknocker clanged.

* * *

"Nazie, you're not a little girl anymore, you just got married—go and bring the food!" An abyss opened in Miriam Hanoum's black eyes, as she rose and came and slammed the door in Nazie's face.

Nazie opened the door a crack and pushed in a muddy white shoe. "It's not there, *ameh bozorg,* by my life...," she whispered, and displayed her sooty hands by way of proof.

"So where did the chickens with the raisins and carrots fly to, Nazie? All right, come in now, come in...If it wasn't for the vow I made your mother—come in, and cover your ears so people won't see." The kerchief and the veil were transparent from the rain, and her dress trailed behind her like a moth-eaten rag. When she came into the room, the wineglasses stopped clinking together, and the guests' loud congratulations to the family fell silent. They looked at Nazie pityingly, at her wet dress, her slipping feather breasts, and forgot that she was Moussa's wife and remembered Nazichi the orphan.

"Homa, you go to the *comejdoun,* seeing that our bride is incapable of finding a pot of chickens buried in the ground!" Miriam Hanoum roared over Nazie's slumped shoulders, and Homa limped out.

"But there really isn't anything there, *ameh bozorg.*"

Nazie's legs trembled under her dress, and she needed to pee. "The ground ate up everything…"

Then Homa came back into the house with the pot full of bare chicken bones, and all the guests rose and gathered in a semicircle at the door.

"Homa, damn your eyes, you've eaten all the food!" shrieked Miriam Hanoum, her eyes popping out of her head.

"No, ma, no." Homa flapped her arms in terror, causing drops of rain and chicken bones to fly in all directions. "It was Fathaneh Delkasht who ate it all, by my life!" The pot fell on the floor with a loud bang and rolled noisily. "She threw the pot over the almond trees and said that all the curses that you cursed her and her sister, ma, should come down on us—it was like a thousand demons were talking from her throat."

"*Ptui!*" Miriam Hanoum spat in alarm. "*Ptui!*"

"And then she said, 'Your mother slaughtered fat chickens for the miserable wedding she made for Nazichi and Moussa,' and she was laughing with snorts like Manijoun, and she said that if you tell people that she and her children and peacocks ate our food, she would go tomorrow to *mullah* Hassan and cancel the marriage, because the poor little girl doesn't have her period, not even breasts, she said, and father will spend a hundred days in prison because of the bribe he gave the *mullah*. By my life, ma, it's all true, and she said that Flora—oh, the things she said about Flor…"

"Shut up, Homa, shut up now!" Moussa roared, waving his hands in the air. His mother cursed and swore, and the embarrassed guests departed, because the sweet stories that rabbi *mullah* Netanel offered them in place of the stuffed chickens did not satisfy their appetites, and he, too, left.

Nazie lay in her uncle and aunt's room, behind the closed door, trembling and containing herself not to pee. Miriam Hanoum stroked her face, but her eyes kept wandering to the window. She took the white kerchief from Nazie's head, passed her fingers through the disheveled hair, and wiped off the mud that had spattered the girl's face. Then she bent down and, sighing, removed the white laquered shoes and rubbed Nazie's feet with her warm hands.

"Please don't leave me now." Nazie clutched Miriam Hanoum's arm, because she desperately longed for her mother.

"No, *azizam,* don't be afraid..." Miriam Hanoum pulled away.

"Please, please, don't leave me alone, I want to come with you, please, *ameh bozorg,* please." Fresh tears flowed from Nazie's eyes, and her hands did not loosen their grip on Miriam Hanoum's arms.

"Enough, Nazie! It's not nice what you're doing, you're not a little girl anymore—soon you'll be *kuchik madar*—sit on the bed and wait for your husband to come in."

"Stay with me..." Nazie pressed her thighs together.

"Come now, stop crying, enough!...God have mercy on Flora, she's such an idiot. She told you what Shahin—God send him to hell—what he did to her that night, didn't she?"

Nazie nodded. The copper plates that Homa was stacking in the kitchen made a loud ringing noise, and Miriam Hanoum blew out the candle with one puff.

"Well, I hope God gives you both better luck than my daughters—and He should pour boiling black tar into the heart of stinking Fathaneh," Miriam Hanoum shouted, closing the door behind her. "And blood, blood should flow like water all year round from Sultana's hole, *hoy Khodaiah,* please God!"

Moussa came in and at once kissed Nazie's lips. His eyes were shut, and his lips tinkled on hers like a teaspoon stirring sugar in a glass of tea. Putting his hand to the front of her dress, he unbuttoned it slowly, until the damp feather breasts fell out with the strip of bedsheet and rolled on the floor. He tickled her with his fingers. Nazie giggled, and the stream of urine that flowed into her underpants spread a pleasant warmth between her thighs. Moussa did not notice the odorous circle that spread slowly through her damp dress. He only opened his eyes and saw Nazie laughing in the dark when he heard his mother's jubilant voice shouting:

"Well, you finished, Moussa, you finished there?" Miriam Hanoum thumped on the door enthusiastically. "You two finished now?"